Robert Grant

The bachelor's Christmas, and other stories

Robert Grant

The bachelor's Christmas, and other stories

ISBN/EAN: 9783337261887

Printed in Europe, USA, Canada, Australia, Japan

Cover: Foto ©Andreas Hilbeck / pixelio.de

More available books at **www.hansebooks.com**

The Bachelor's Christmas
And Other Stories

The Bachelor's Christmas and Other Stories. By Robert Grant

Illustrated by C. D. Gibson, I. R. Wiles
A. B. Wenzell, and C. Carleton

Charles Scribner's Sons
New York ~~~~ 1895

TROW DIRECTORY
PRINTING AND BOOKBINDING COMPANY
NEW YORK

TROW DIRECTORY
PRINTING AND BOOKBINDING COMPANY
NEW YORK

CONTENTS

LIST OF ILLUSTRATIONS

  LIST OF ILLUSTRATIONS

THE BACHELOR'S
CHRISTMAS

THE BACHELOR'S CHRISTMAS

I

THOMAS WIGGIN, or Tom Wiggin, as everyone called him, sat alone in his bachelor quarters on Christmas-eve, waiting for a carriage. The carriage was not late, but Tom, who was a methodical man in everything he did, had finished his preparations a little sooner than need be. His fur coat and hat and gloves lay on a chair beside him, ready to put on the moment Bridget, the maid, should knock at the door and tell him that Perkins, the cabby at the corner, was blocking the way. Tom had already taken out of his pocket two ten-dollar gold pieces and laid them on the centre-table beside an array of packages done up with marvellous care in the whitest of paper and the reddest of ribbon. One of the gold pieces was for Bridget and the other for Perkins. Twice the sum would not have replaced the crockery and objects of virtu which the Hibernian hand-maiden, who brought up his breakfast and was supposed to keep his room tidy, had smashed since he had tipped her last; and Tom had, only two months before, under-gone the melancholy experience of falling through the bottom of Perkins's coupé, be-cause of the pertinacity with which that common carrier of passengers clung to the delusion that no repairs to a vehicle were necessary until it dropped to pieces. But as Tom would have said if interrogated on the subject by a subtler mind, Christmas comes but once a year, and though Bridget's best was her worst, she had tried to do it, and Perkins, shiftless as he was, had driven his poor old nag one day into a pink lather in endeavoring to catch a train for him, which he had just missed after all.

Besides, Tom had had a remarkably good business year, so that a ten-dollar gold piece did not seem to him the dazzlingly large sum he had regarded it ten years earlier. He had lived in these same bachelor lodgings for ten years, and during that time had built up a very neat business by his own unaided effort, as his contemporaries (and contemporaries are apt to be stern critics) were ready to admit. He had worked hard and steadily, taking only enough vacation to enable him to keep well, and shunting everything to the background which threatened to interfere with the object he had in view—that is, everything but one thing. And this one thing he had made up his mind five years ago was out of the question. Consequently he had shunted it to the background with everything else, and devoted himself more unreservedly than ever to the real estate business.

Ten years is quite a piece out of any man's life, and though Tom Wiggin was the picture of health, he was, as we say colloquially, no longer a chicken. He was stouter than he had been and had lost some of his hair, which gave him rather a middle-aged appearance, or at least suggested that he never would see thirty-five again. When he had taken his present room he had been a slim and almost delicate-looking stripling without a copper, whom any girl might be likely to fancy. To-day, in his own estimation and in that of his friends and acquaintances, he was a well-seasoned old bachelor who was not likely to ask any one feminine to share his comfortable competency.

Christmas comes but once a year, and Tom had for several years past been in the habit of recognizing the fact in his special way. He was extensively an uncle. That is to say, he had two married sisters, one with five and the other with three children of tender age, and each of his two married brothers had present-ed him with a nephew and niece of the name of Wiggin. Categorically speaking, he had seven nephews and five nieces to provide with Christmas gifts, not to mention his two sisters and his two sisters-in-law, all of whom had grown accustomed to expect a package in white paper tied with pink rib-bon and marked "with love and a merry Christmas from Tom." Here were sixteen presents to begin with, and there were apt to be almost as many more. On this particular Christmas evening there were thirty-five par-cels in all, each done up with immaculate care, for Tom, like most other bachelors, prided himself on doing everything in a thor-ough, deliberate fashion. He had made his last purchase a fortnight ago, and had spent two entire evenings in putting the array of toys and fancy goods in presentable order. They were of all sorts and sizes, for Tom had paled neither before bulk nor price. There was a safety bicycle for a nephew who had set his heart on one, and the tiniest of gold watches for his eldest niece. There was a warm, fur-lined cloak for his dead mother's oldest friend, a spinster lady who had small means wherewith to keep herself comfortable in a cold world, and a case of marvellous port for his old chum, Belden, who would see that it was not wasted on unappreciative palates. Everything was ready for the summons from Perkins, the cabby, and Tom, bald-headed bachelor that he was, was fuming a little in spite of the fact that it still lacked three minutes of the hour appointed for departure.

The clock in the neighboring church tower, whose tones were plainly audible in the sky parlors which he called his home, had only just struck five when the tramp of feet followed by a knock announced the joint arrival of Bridget and Perkins, to whom he had intrusted the duty of helping him to carry his precious parcels down three flights of stairs

to the attendant cab. This was the sixth
consecutive year Bridget and Perkins had
done the same thing, and they thought they
knew what to expect. But they had counted without their host. A year ago they
had chuckled for forty-eight hours over a
five-dollar bill apiece. Now, when they
opened the door and presented their grinning countenances, their benefactor, after
shouting at them a merry Christmas, proceeded to daze their intellects, of every par-
ticle of which they stood in sore need for the
purpose of a safe descent, by tossing to each
of them a gold coin of twice the denomina-
tion. For some moments they stood in bewildered, sheepish silence, examining their
treasure, as though to make certain it was
genuine ; then Bridget, taxing her intelligence for a suitable expression for the wealth
of feeling at her heart, exclaimed :

" And sure, Mr. Wiggin, it's Bridget Lan-
agan that's hoping that before the good Lord
brings anither Christmas-day the proudest
lady in the land will be yer wife. It's me
and Perkins would be the first to say 'God
bless her,' though we lost a good job by it."
At this prodigal outburst of expectation Tom

Wiggin's countenance grew rosy-red, notwithstanding the incredulous laugh with which he received the blessing of his warm-hearted handmaiden and the nods of the less nimble-witted cab-man. Then a shadow crossed it as though of unhappy recollection, and there was a tinge of real hopelessness in his half-jocular protestation.

"Many thanks, Bridget, for your good wishes, but there's no such luck in store for me. I shall live and die an old bachelor such as you see me now, and you and Perkins will be able to count on a ten-dollar gold piece on Christmas-eve for the rest of your lives. That is," Tom added by way of timely warning, "provided you don't smash any of these things of mine in carrying them down-stairs. You remember that the pair of you last year between you broke a teacup worth its weight in gold, and the year before that large vase broke itself. If everything were to go down safely I should almost begin to believe that what Bridget hopes might come true. Careful now, and be sure not to lay that bicycle right on top of the gilt-edged dinner-plates for my sister Mary."

Whether it was that Tom's strictures in regard to the clumsiness of his assistants were exaggerated, or they were bent on causing him to repose trust in Bridget's prophecy, the thirty-five packages reached the cab and were stowed within and without, under their owner's supervising eye, without a single casualty.

"Faith, Mr. Wiggin, they'll be taking yer this time for Santa Claus, sure," said Perkins when the last precious parcel had been deposited. "Yer'll have to ride outside, sir, as yer did last year."

Evidently the gaping file of small boys which had formed itself on each side of the doorway was of the opinion that, if the gentleman in the fur coat was not Santa Claus, he was one of his blood-relations, for, as Tom climbed carefully to his post beside Perkins so as not to hazard the safety of the bicycle and the box of port, for which there was no room inside, they broke out into a shrill hurrah. Perhaps they too, or at least some of them, knew what they had to expect, for before Santa Claus seated himself on the box he plunged his hands into the side pockets of his fur overcoat, and then reproducing them, seemed to toss them high to the winds, as he cried, with gay good-will :

"Scramble now, you little devils, scramble, and wish you merry Christmas!"

What Tom flung to the winds was neither his fingers nor his thumbs, but a plethora of bright nickels which he had drawn from the bank for the express purpose. As the glittering shower of brand-new five-cent pieces fell to the icy sidewalk, the band of urchins threw themselves upon it with a shout of transport which drew tears from the eyes of the tender-hearted Bridget, who had remained to witness this established ceremony, and ought to have warmed the cockles of the donor's heart, if indeed they needed warming. Twice again he replunged his hands into his pockets and twice again the yell was repeated. Then seating himself beside Perkins, Tom gave the signal for departure, and as the cab rounded the corner a score of little lungs gave him back his merry Christmas with all their might.

It was a genuine Christmas-eve. The ground was covered with snow and the sleigh-bells were jangling merrily. The lamps were already lighted, and many a parlor window gave out the reflection of wreaths of holly, and now and again sparkled with little rows of candles in token of the precious Christmas anniversary. Perkins's coupé was on wheels, and his equine paradox was imperfectly caulked into the bargain, so that the world seemed to be rushing by them as they jogged along. Tom had a list which he from time to time consulted by the allied light of the moon and the street-lamps, in order to see that his itinerary was accurately followed and no one forgotten. At every house he dismounted in person and handed in his present. When he reached the residence of his sister, Mary Ferris, who was the mother of the five children, he had to make four trips up and down the door-steps. His sister, who was listening, recognized his voice and came into the vestibule to meet him, and her children, bounding in her wake like an elated pack of wolves, shouted with one tongue,

"Hurrah! it's Uncle Tom."

Mrs. Ferris sent them scampering upstairs in double-quick time on pain of dire penalties if they peeped or listened, and fondly drew her brother into the small sitting-room which opened out of the hall.

"I can't stop, Mary," he said; "I'm on my

annual circuit. Now let's see if I've got everything. Here's the bicycle for Roger, junior. They call it 'a safety,' and I trust it may prove so. And the Noah's ark, the largest one made, for Harry; and a musical box, which plays eight tunes, for Dorothy; and a doll which sings 'Ta-ra-boom-de-ay' for little Mary; and a woolly lamb for baby Ned. And here's a trifle in the crockery line for you, my dear. If you don't like the pattern you can change them. Now I must be off. How's Roger, senior? Give him my love and a merry Christmas."

"He'll be at home very soon, Tom, and dreadfully sorry to have missed you. The children are just crazy about their stockings, and little Roger had given up all hope of a bicycle. You are too generous to them and to all of us. And, oh, Tom," she added, laying her hand upon his arm, "I feel dreadfully that we shan't have you with us at dinner to-morrow, but old Mr. Ferris depends on Roger and me for Christmas. He says it may be the last time, and that Christmas is the Ferris day. Thanksgiving is the Wiggin day, you know, and we did have a jolly time then; yet I just hate to think of your not dining with one of us on Christmas. How can it be helped, though, if all the things-in-law have family parties?"

"Why, that's all right, Mary. As you say, Thanksgiving is the Wiggin day, and things-in-law have rights, as well as those they marry. Merry Christmas, dearest, and let me go, or I shall never get through my list."

"Ah, but, Tom love, I do wish you were married," she cried, putting her arms around his neck to detain him. She was his favorite sister, and free to introduce dangerous topics with due discretion. "You would be so much happier."

"Do I seem so miserable?" he inquired, as he looked down at her and stroked her hair. "That's an old story, Mary. I've heard you express the same wish every six months for the last ten years. Every family should have one old bachelor, at least, and I shall be ours."

She was silent for an instant. "Do you ever see Isabelle Hardy, nowadays?" she asked, with brave insistence. "I have sometimes thought"—she stopped, deterred from completing her sentence by the shadow which had come over Tom's face.

He gently, but firmly, removed his sister's arms from his neck, and answered gravely, almost stiffly, "Very rarely indeed." Then, with a fresh access of gayety, as though he were resolved that nothing foreign to the occasion should mar its spirit, he cried lustily, "A merry Christmas to you, Mary!" and departed.

Continuing steadily on his round, Tom delivered safely the case of port, and the fur-lined cloak, and brought up in the next street, in front of his brother Joe's house. Here he was to leave the gold watch for his eldest niece, a generous box of bonbons for his sister-in-law, a tool-chest for young Joe, and a first edition of "Vanity Fair" for Joe himself, who, though not particularly well off, was a rabid book collector. Tom had dogged an auctioneer for two days to make sure of obtaining the volume in question, which, so far as he could see, was like as two peas to the subsequent issues of the same book to be bought anywhere for a song. He was convinced of his mistake when he saw his brother's face light up at sight of the treasure-trove and heard his delighted inquiry, "Where on earth did you pick this up, Tom?

You couldn't have given me anything I'd rather have."

"Glad you like it, Joe. If it isn't the real thing, I'll have the hide of that fellow, Nevins, who sold it to me."

"The real thing? It's a genuine first edition and a splendid specimen. It's adorable. I say, old fellow, it's an outrage that we're to dine with Julia's father to-morrow and leave you out in the cold. Another year I mean to strike and have a Wiggin Christmas dinner, Thanksgiving or no Thanksgiving. Mary and I were comparing notes yesterday, and vowing it was an infernal shame."

"Now, it's all right as it is, Joe. I've just left Mary, and I understand perfectly. You've got enough to do to digest your father-in-law's mince pie and Madeira without having me on your stomach."

"A regular old-fashioned ten-course feed, where you sit down at seven and get up at half-past ten feeling like lead. Ugh! Where are you going to dine, Tom?"

"No matter. That's my secret. I shall have a good dinner, never you fear. I must be off now and deliver the rest of my goods."

"It's an outrage—an infernal outrage,"

growled Joe. "Before you go, old man," he said, hooking his arm into his brother's, and dragging him in the direction of the dining-room, "we'll have a drink. I put a pint of fizz on the ice this morning for your special benefit. It won't take two minutes to mix the cock-tail." Thereupon Joe gave the bell-handle a wrench, and directed that the bottle in the ice-chest should be brought up together with the cracked ice which he had ordered to be in readiness, and in a very short space of time the white-capped maid reappeared with a waiter laden with all the necessary ingredients for the delectable beverage in question. Joe carefully measured out some bitters, pop went the cork of the Perrier Jouet, and presently the brothers were looking at each other over two brimming glasses.

"Wish you merry Christmas, Joe."

"Wish you merry Christmas, Tom. And here's to *her*." Joe paused an instant before he drank to add, "It's a big mistake you're not married, Tom. All I can say is some girl is losing a first-class husband. I say here's to *her*."

Tom, who had waited at the words, raised

2

his glass solemnly. "There is no her and there never will be," he said, with quiet decision. "Still, since you give the toast, Joe, I'll drink it. It's not poisonous," he added, with a wry smile—"so here's to *her*." He drained his glass and set it down on the waiter, then for an instant stood ruminantly with his back to the open fire. "The drink was better than the toast in my case, Joe. My her must have died in infancy."

"Honest Injun, Tom?" asked Joe, as he gripped his brother's hand held out for a parting shake and looked into his face.

Tom's eyes quailed before the honest gaze. His lip quivered. "I'm an infernal liar, Joe, and you know it. But what's the use? She wouldn't have me, man—and there's no one else whom I want to have. So, merry Christmas, Joe, and God bless you and yours."

As he went out into the frosty night the clock in the hall struck half-past six. There were only five parcels left and the coupé was nearly empty. Tom opened the door and stepping inside, lay back wearily. Presently he picked up one of the parcels—it was a book apparently, from its shape—and laid it at his side. When Perkins drew up the next time, Tom gathered up the remaining four and ran up the steps with them. They were for his sister Kitty and her little company, and he spent a few moments indoors to explain matters. When he reappeared he said to his conductor, " 114 Farragut Place, and then to the Club."

Tom sat inside with the remaining package resting on his lap, nervously watching for the cab to stop. They halted presently before a spacious house, the old-fashioned aspect of which was heightened by the curved iron railing which ran along the flight of steps leading up to it. Just before the cab stopped Tom had taken a note from his breast pocket, and, after looking round him stealthily in the darkness, had kissed the envelope. Now he tucked it under the red ribbon of the remaining package, and walking gravely up the steps, rang the bell. There was nothing in the envelope but his visiting card, on which he had written, " with best wishes for a merry Christmas." When the servant came to the door Tom said, " Will you please give this to Miss Isabelle Hardy." Then the door closed in his face and he went solemnly down the steps again. On reaching the now empty cab he glanced over his shoulder as though in hope of catching a face at the window, but every shade was down, and the wreaths of holly were the nearest semblance to faces, and they seemed almost to grin at him. And well they might. It was the fifth year in succession that he had gone through exactly this same pantomime. Tom heaved one deep sigh; then he straightened his shoulders and passed his hand across his eyes as though he were sweeping away an unprofitable vision.

"To the club," he repeated sturdily to Perkins. "And now," he said to himself, as he shrouded himself in his fur coat and put up his feet on the opposite cushion, "the question is how to make the best of a devilish poor outlook. I mean to have a merry Christmas somehow."

II

Though it was dinner time, there were few men in the club when Tom entered it. Still there was a half-dozen familiar spirits lounging in the sitting-room, most melancholy

THE WREATHS OF HOLLY WERE THE NEAREST SEMBLANCE TO
FACES, AND THEY SEEMED ALMOST TO GRIN AT HIM

among whom was Frazer Bell, a bachelor far gone in the forties, an epicure, but poor as a church mouse.

"Just the man," said Tom to himself, and he drew him aside.

"Will you dine with me to-night, Frazer?"

"Er—I have just ordered dinner, but——"

"Then I'll countermand it," interposed Tom blithely, by way of relieving his would-be guest from the quandary of accepting the invitation without loss of self-respect. "It's Christmas-eve and this is my outfit; I'm going in for as good a dinner as they can give us in honor of the occasion. I say, old man, will you do me the favor to order it? You know fifty times better than I what we ought to have to get the best."

Frazer Bell grinned melodiously. One could almost see his mouth water.

"I'll do it if you like," he said.

"I wish you would. And be sure to put down the finest there is, and to pick out something gilt-edged in the way of wine; something cobwebby and precious."

"I'll try," said Frazer, with another grin, and he ambled off in the direction of the office.

Tom went into the reading-room and picked up a magazine. Presently he passed his hands across his eyes again, for the wreaths in the windows of the house in Farragut Place were grinning at him still. He said to himself that he guessed he needed another drink, and pressed the electric button at his side.

"Ask Mr. Frazer Bell what he'll have and bring me a Martini cocktail," he said to the servant. Then he shut his eyes and the grinning wreaths changed into a girl's face, a face which had haunted him day in and day out for seven years. He knew that he ought to brush that away also, but he could not bring himself to do it on Christmas-eve. He would give himself that little luxury at least, before he tried to obliterate it by talking gastronomy with Frazer Bell. Nearly seven years, verily, since he had seen her first! She was then a girl of nineteen, and he at the bottom of the real estate ladder without a dollar to his name, as it were. He had been crazy to marry her, and for two years he had followed her from ball-room to ball-room with a feverish assiduity which threatened to revolutionize his business habits and make light of his business principles. He was not the only one in love with her; there were half a dozen; but the one whose devotion he dreaded most was Charles Leverett Saunders, a handsome dashing beau, a scion of a rich and conspicuous house. He had watched her behavior toward his rival with the eye of a lynx, and as he compared the notes of one evening with the notes of the next he had felt that she was more gracious to Saunders than to him. And yet sometimes she was so sweet and kind to him. But then, again she would be cold and distant, almost icy, in short; on which occasions he had felt as though he would like to cut his throat. A half-dozen times he had made up his mind to offer himself to her and know his fate, but somehow his determination, which was so prodigious in other affairs, had failed him. So matters had gone for a year and a half, and he had seemed no nearer and no less near to the goal than ever. He had said to himself severely that this thing must not go on.

On December 31st, just five years ago, there was to be a famous ball, the crack party of the season. He had resolved that before the old year was out he would know his fate once and for all. Ten-dollar gold pieces did not grow for him then on every bush, but he ordered from the florist the handsomest bouquet of roses and violets which native horticultural talent could devise, and sent it to Miss Isabelle Hardy on the eve of the ball. She had promised to dance the German with him, and when he entered the ball-room his eyes saw no one until they rested on her. A frown had creased his brow, for she was on the arm of Charles Leverett Saunders, and was looking up into his face with a smile of happy excitement which had suggested to Tom that he was as far from her thoughts as the Emperor of Japan. What was more and worse, she carried three gorgeous bouquets, but his was not among them. Where was it? Had it not been sent? If so, he would ruin that florist's trade for ever and ever. Or had she left it at home on purpose?

He fought shy of her until the German and there was no longer an excuse for him to keep away. Almost at once she thanked him for his lovely flowers.

" But you have not brought them."

"No," she said, sweetly. "I was unable to— I," and she had paused in her embarrassment.

"There were so many, of course."

"No, it was not that, Mr. Wiggin, I assure you." But she had looked a little hurt at his gruff words. "I had a very good reason for not bringing them."

There had been a piteous look in the girl's eyes as she spoke, which he had often recalled since; but then he had thought of nothing but his anger and the slight which had been put upon him. He felt like asking why she had not left Charles Leverett Saunders's flowers at home instead of his. It was clear that she did not care for him, and it became clearer and clearer in the course of the evening; for after a while they had sat almost tongue-tied beside each other. He had tried his best not to be disagreeable, but in spite of himself cynical sentences had slipped from between his teeth in close succession. He had seen that she was hurt and he had rather gloried in it, and presently an embarrassed silence had followed, broken by the arrival of his rival with a magnificent favor proffered beamingly to the girl of Tom's heart. She had sailed away, and looking back over her shoulder, given Tom one glance —one of those icy glances which made him yearn to cut his throat. That was bad enough, but to crown all, when her turn came to bestow a boutonnière she made Tom carry her straight up to Leverett Saunders, in the button-hole of whose coat she proceeded to fasten the rosebud for which Tom would have given twelve months of his life.

Five years ago on the first of January! He had gone home that night certain that Isabelle Hardy did not love him, and resolved that she should play fast and loose with him no longer. In the first hours of the new year he vowed that he would forget her, and devote himself to his business heart and soul. Henceforth he would close eye and brain to all distractions. He would cease forever to be a plaything for a woman's caprice.

He had kept his word. That is to say, his attentions had ended from that hour. The festivities which had known him knew him no more. He went nowhere, and the reason whispered under the rose was that Isabelle Hardy had given him the mitten. The whisper reached him, but little he cared that rumor was not strictly accurate. Was it not practically so? She had to all intents and

ONE OF THOSE ICY GLANCES WHICH MADE HIM YEARN TO CUT HIS THROAT

purposes thrown him over, and he had expelled her image from his heart and gone on with his business, looking neither to the right nor to the left. Occasionally he passed her in the street, and on every Christmas-eve since the night of his resolution, he had left a trifling remembrance at the house in Farragut Place, just, as it were, to show that there was no ill feeling. Otherwise they never met, and here he was to-day, an old bachelor close on forty, getting bald and set in his ways, with a splendid business and a secret ache at his heart. And she? Tom had never known why she had not married Charles Leverett Saunders, as everybody expected and said she was going to do. Yet suddenly, without warning, that dashing gallant had gone abroad and had remained there ever since, doing the Nile, and Norway, and hunting tigers in the jungles of India, according as the humor seized him. And she? She was beginning to show just a little the traces of time, to suggest what she would look like if she never married and remained after all an old maid. He had been struck by it the last time he had passed her in the street. An old maid!

Isabelle Hardy an old maid! There was bitter humor in it for Tom, and he laughed aloud in the reading-room, then, starting at his own performance, looked around him confusedly. He was alone, and his untasted drink stood at his elbow. No one had heard his harsh, strange outburst. He tossed off the cocktail and sank back in his easy chair to confront the vision. An old maid. And he was an old bachelor. And it was Christmas-eve. And what a gloomy, diabolical anniversary it was for old maids and old bachelors. They had no things-in-law to invite them to dinner. They were out in the cold and their room was better than their company. Jokes? Jollities? They were all matrimonial and centred about baby's teeth or Noah's arks. The only thing for an old bachelor or old maid to do was to ransack toy shops and then stand aside. Merry Christmas? How in the name of Santa Claus was an old bachelor or an old maid to have a merry Christmas? And why in time shouldn't they be merry if they could?

Five minutes later, the servant had to announce twice that dinner was served before Tom turned his head, which caused that functionary to reflect that Mr. Wiggin was getting a little deaf. He was looking straight before him into the fire, as though he were interested in the processes of combustion or the price of coal. He turned at the second summons with a start.

"What's that, Simon? Mr. Bell waiting for me? Oh, of course; dinner is ready. Tell him—tell him," he added with a feverish, excited manner as he sprang to his feet, "that I'll be with him in a moment. I must use the telephone first. I'll put it through," he added to himself as he dashed from the room, "if it takes a leg."

Whatever Tom was bent on almost cost him a bone of some sort at the start, for just beyond the door of the reading-room he bumped full into George Hapgood, a stout, dignified-looking man of about fifty. When Tom realized who it was his eyes gleamed joyously, and in lieu of an apology he blurted out:

"You're just the man I'm looking for, Hapgood. Will you do me the favor to dine with me to-morrow? Now don't say you can't, for you must."

"To-morrow? To-morrow's Christmas,

isn't it?" was the inquiry, with just a shade of melancholy in the tone.

"Yes. And we're out of it—two old bachelors like you and me. I'm going to bring a few choice spirits together to prove that the things-in-law can't have all the fun. Say you'll come. Here, at seven."

"I—I was going to dine with my brother, but I got a telegram from him this afternoon saying that the children had broken out with scarlet fever and——"

"I understand, old man. So did mine. I mean—we're all in the same boat. Then I shall count on you at seven."

"Thank you kindly, Wiggin. I'll be glad to come," answered Hapgood, with a grave, courteous bow. Tom remembered having heard it said that Hapgood had never really smiled since his lady-love, Marian Blake, married Willis Bolles, twenty-five years before. He was a brilliant lawyer and an influential man, but he had never been known to smile, and he habitually fought shy of all entertainments where the other sex was to be encountered, as though he feared contagion.

"I thought I wouldn't tell him that there might be women. It 'll do him good to meet a few," chuckled Tom, as he pursued his way to the telephone box.

"Is that Albion Hall?"

"Yes, seh."

"Is Mr. Maxwell there?"

"No, seh, Mr. Maxwell has gone home."

"Who are you?"

"The janitor, seh."

"Is the hall engaged for to-morrow night?"

"Can't say, seh. Haven't any orders. You mean Christmas night, seh?"

"Yes, to-morrow, Christmas."

"Likely not, seh."

"Where does Mr. Maxwell live?"

"Plainville, seh."

"Humph! Do you wish to make a ten-dollar bill, janitor? Very well. Take a carriage and drive out to Plainville as tight as you can fetch it, and find out if Mr. Thomas Wiggin—he knows me—can have the hall to-morrow night. Tell Mr. Maxwell that if he'll meet me at my rooms at eight o'clock to-morrow, Christmas morning, I'll add twenty-five per cent. to the price. Do you understand? Now repeat what I've said to you. That's right. Go along now and report to me at the Blackstone Club as soon as you get back, and for every five minutes which you take from an hour and a half I'll add an extra dollar to the ten."

Tom looked at his watch reflectively. It was a quarter past seven. He must dine first, if only not to break faith with Frazer Bell, whom he had kept waiting abominably long already. He stopped an instant, however, at the office on his way to join Frazer, so as to make sure that he could have the large green dining-room for the following evening.

"To-morrow's Christmas, you know, Mr. Wiggin?" suggested the steward, respectfully.

"I know it, Dunklee. Is there any reason why I shouldn't give a dinner party on Christmas day?"

"No, sir, of course not. I merely thought that perhaps you were going to dine elsewhere and had forgotten it was Christmas day."

"I dine here, and—I wish a dinner for, say sixteen—I can't tell the precise number yet— a ladies' dinner. And I wish it to be as handsome as possible. You mustn't fail me," he added, noticing that the steward looked rather dismayed. "Start your messengers at once and spare no expense, if you have to drag the butchers from their beds to get what you need. I'll see to the flowers myself; I have a greenhouse in my mind's eye which I intend to buy solidly for the occasion."

"Very well, Mr. Wiggin, I'll do my best, though it's late to begin, sir."

Frazer Bell was sitting before his raw oysters the picture of polite despair, seeing in his mind's eye the delicate dinner which he had ordered being done to death and getting lukewarm.

" My dear fellow, I owe you a thousand pardons, but I had to telephone. If our dinner is spoiled, or whether it is or not, I want you to promise to dine with me to-morrow night. I have evolved a scheme while we were waiting, which I will unfold to you presently. Go on with your oysters. I hope you will forgive me."

" To-morrow, Christmas ? "

" Yes. I propose to give an entertainment to all the old bachelors and maiden ladies of my acquaintance, if they'll come. A dinner here followed by a dance at Albion Hall, and Dunklee is arranging for the dinner. I'm going to invite all the old timers, and I need your advice as to the list. For a starter I'll put down the three Bellknap girls."

Tom whipped out his pencil and proceeded to utilize the back of the bill of fare which Frazer had had drawn up to gloat over.

"See first what you're going to eat, old man."

"It's sure to be admirable if you ordered it. It has always been a matter of wonder to me that neither of those Bellknap girls have married. Then there's Georgiana Dixon, in the same block. Glad I remembered her. Charming girl too. She ought to have been married years ago. Come to think of it, you used to be a friend of hers, Frazer."

"Yes, I did. What on earth are you up to, Tom? Are you in earnest?"

"Never more so in my life. I tell you there's a tacit conspiracy in this town—I dare say it's all over the planet—against us poor wretches who are old enough to be married and haven't, and they—the married ones I mean—like to keep us out in the cold, as a sort of punishment, may be, because we've chosen to remain single. I'm sick of it for one, and I'm going to organize a revolution.

I'm going to have a grand family meeting of all the poor lonely spirits like you and me and the Bellknap girls and Georgiana Dixon and George Hapgood, and—and the things-in-law may go to the devil. Now put your wits on this thing, Frazer, while you disintegrate your terrapin. Come, girls first."

"Do you suppose they'll ever come? " asked Frazer, with an amazed grin. He was essentially a conventional man without a spark of imagination, and he could scarcely believe that Tom was really in earnest.

"They've got to come. Why shouldn't they come? "

"They'll think it queer."

" It isn't queer. It's righteous."

"All right. Put down Miss Mamie Scott. She will never see thirty again."

"Capital. Poor soul! A girl to make any man happy."

" There's Susan Davis."

"To be sure. She isn't pretty, but she's good. Joe Elliott used to be partial to her before he ran a rig with that smug-faced doll who jilted him. What a fool he was! We'll ask him too."

To tell the truth, even the gastronomic

Frazer Bell, in spite of the fact that the dinner was very far from spoiled, presently forgot what he was eating and drinking in the absorbing process of selection. By the time the cheese and a rare glass of Burgundy arrived the list was finished, and Tom was eager to escape to the reading-room to prepare the notes of invitation, which must be sent at once. There were forty-six in all to be invited, out of which he hoped to secure enough for a full-fledged dinner party. Those who could not come to dinner were to be urged to join them at Albion Hall later.

The matter of wording the invitation was a serious one, and Tom sat feeling of the bald spot on his crown for several minutes. At last, with a desperate air he plunged his pen into the inkstand and wrote as follows to Miss Madeline Bellknap:

"MY DEAR MISS BELLKNAP: I beg as a favor that you and both your sisters will honor me with your company at dinner to-morrow, December 25th, at the Blackstone Club, at seven o'clock. I am bringing together, in celebration of a bachelor's Christmas, a number of kindred spirits who have no things-in-law to cater to their sympathetic needs, and yet who have a no less equal right to a merry Christmas. After dinner we shall adjourn to Albion Hall to dance, to which I trust that you or some of you, if unable to dine with me, will come at ten o'clock. With the compliments of the season and the sincere hope that you will oblige me, I am,

" Very sincerely yours,

" THOMAS WIGGIN."

" How is that, Frazer ? "

" I guess it's all right," said Frazer, in a tone which suggested that he was far from sure whether it was not all wrong.

" Perfectly respectful and to the point, isn't it ? "

" Yes. Hold on, Tom. How about a chaperon ? They won't come without a chaperon."

Tom bit his lip. " I won't have a chaperon. I'll be —— if I will have a chaperon." He puckered his brow gloomily ; then, with a sudden wave of his hand, he cried,

" I have it."

Thereupon he dashed off this postscript :

" P.S. We are all old enough to take care of ourselves."

For the next two hours Tom and Frazer devoted themselves with feverish industry to the task of writing the two-score invitations. In such an emergency forgery seemed allowable, and, without attempting to imitate the Wiggin chirography, Frazer boldly signed the name of Thomas. As soon as every half-dozen notes were finished they were hurried to their destination by special messengers. The clock struck half-past ten when the last was done. Tom handed over to the boy in attendance the final batch, all save a single one. While he was writing this he could have written half a dozen of the others, and now that it was written and addressed he drew it from the envelope to read once more the words which he had penned so carefully. Their tenor was essentially the same, but he had stricken out a phrase or two here, and added a phrase or two there, to make sure that she would understand the nature of the invitation. Then he arose with it in his hand and said, " Good-night, Frazer. A thousand thanks. I'll leave this one myself. Wish you merry Christmas."

III

At half past six on the evening of Christmas day Tom Wiggin stood in the large green dining-room of the Blackstone Club, surveying a magnificently appointed table. Roses, pansies, and violets from the greenhouse which he had bought out at ten o'clock that morning, lay tastefully banked and scattered upon the cloth, intertwined with masses of evergreen and holly gay with berries. Christmas wreaths and festoons were lavishly arranged around the walls. Dunklee had assured him that there should be no dearth of palatable viands, and, most important fact of all, there had been twenty acceptances for dinner, happily just ten men and ten women, and nearly a dozen more acceptances for the dance. He had been in a mad whirl since daybreak, but he believed now that he had accomplished everything except to arrange the seats at table, which needed a little quiet reflection.

The answers had begun to arrive shortly after breakfast. The first had been a refusal, a little curt and stiff in tone, as though the lady in question, notwithstanding the fact that she had promised to dine with one of her family, wished to give him to understand that she took herself too seriously to accept such an invitation under any circumstances. Tom's heart sank within him, and he said to himself that he had made a mess of it. Five minutes later his features were as complacent as those of a Cheshire cat. The Misses Bellknap were coming, all three of them. They had ordered dinner at home, but were coming notwithstanding, to help Mr. Wiggin pass a merry Christmas and confound the things-in-law.

"They are three noble sports," Tom had said to himself, as he danced around his apartment waving the mildly scented note.

Other answers came thick and fast. Of course many had engagements, but most of these expressed deep regret at their inability to attend, and several who could not come to dinner promised to put in an appearance at the dance. There were a few other chilling refusals. Miss Susan Davis, whom Tom had characterized as not pretty but good, let him perceive very plainly that she considered the invitation indelicate. On the other hand, Miss Mamie Scott, who would never see thirty again, had written him spiritedly that it was a comfort to know that she was old enough to take care of herself, and that she was coming without her mother for the first time in her life.

And she? Tom had not heard until nearly noon, and he had realized, as he held the little neatly sealed note in his hand, that if she were going to fail him his pleasure in the whole business would be utterly gone. His wrist shook as though he had the palsy, and he hated to look. She was coming; yes, she was coming. Her father and mother were going to dine with her brother-in-law, and though she had promised to do the same she thought she would enjoy better the very original dinner to which he had invited her. "And, as you say," she wrote in conclusion, "we are certainly old enough to take care of ourselves." She was coming; yes, she was coming, and whatever happened now, he was going to have a merry Christmas.

And how was he to seat them? It was rather a nice problem. To begin with, Tom sandwiched in George Hapgood between the eldest Miss Bellknap and Miss Mamie Scott, which was as delightful a situation as any man could wish to have. Frazer Bell must go beside Georgiana Dixon, and Harry Abercrombie, who had been dangling for years in the train of Angelina Phillips until everybody was tired, should take her in and have the second Miss Bellknap on his other side. Tom was making pretty good progress, but what really troubled him was whether it would do for him to place Isabelle Hardy next to himself. Would not such a proceeding be quite inconsistent with the vow which he had been living up to for the past five years? What sense would there be in putting himself in the way of temptation, when he knew perfectly well that she did not care a button for him? What use, indeed? And yet, as he said to himself, Christmas comes but once a year, and this was his party, and—and had not she herself stated that they certainly were old enough now to take care of themselves? Why shouldn't he sit next to her? He was no longer the sentimental, hot-headed boy of five years ago. They would enjoy themselves like any other sober bachelor and old maid. It would only be for one evening, and beginning with to-morrow he would stick to his vow as sturdily as ever. Yes, he would take

in the eldest Miss Bellknap, who would be the
oldest woman present, and he would put Isabelle Hardy on his left.

When he had made this important decision
Tom found the arrangement of his other guests
a simple matter, and after one final scrutiniz-
ing, but tolerably contented, glance around
the table, he walked into the ladies' drawing-
room to await the arrival of his company.

Punctually on the stroke of seven, the three
Misses Bellknap swept into the room in a
merry flutter. They were tall bean-poles of
girls, who had naturally a prancing style, and
they were in their very best bib and tucker,
which included great puffed sleeves and nodding plumes in their hair. In one breath
they told Tom that they considered it a grand
idea, that they had been practically nowhere
for years, and that it was a real pleasure to be
thought of and taken down from the shelf, if
only for a single evening. It was evident that
they had come determined to have at least a
good time, if not a riot, for when their eyes
rested on George Hapgood standing in the
door-way the picture of blank amazement, all
three giggled convulsively as though they
were eighteen.

"Come in, George, don't be afraid," said Tom. "They won't bite."

"We really won't hurt you, Mr. Hapgood," said Miss Madeline, the eldest; "do come in."

It was too late for the woman-hater to draw back now, so, like the man he was, he braced his muscles and faced the music. He bowed with grave courtesy to the youngest Miss Bellknap; he bowed with a faint smile—just a ghostly glimmer, but, nevertheless, a smile—to Miss Arabella, the second Miss Bellknap; and when he faced the eldest Miss Bellknap, who happening to be the furthest away from him was the last to be reached, his features broke down completely, and he positively laughed—laughed for the first time in twenty years.

"Do shake hands, Mr. Hapgood," said Miss Madeline; "this is like old times."

And now everybody began to arrive in a bunch in the midst of a general handshaking and chorus of merriment. The arrival of each old stager, masculine or feminine, was greeted with fresh exclamations of delight, and a spirit of contagious frivolity was rampant from the very start.

Tom was already bubbling over with enjoyment, but his eyes were glued on the doorway. There she was at last, looking—yes, looking younger and prettier than he had ever seen her in his life, and dressed bewitchingly. An old maid! It was impossible. It was monstrous.

"It was very good of you to come, Miss Hardy."

"I am very much pleased to be here, Mr. Wiggin."

Most conventional phraseology, and there was really no reason why Tom should keep repeating the words over to himself in a dazed sort of fashion until he was called to account by the opening of the doors.

"Dinner is served, sir."

Then readjusting his faculties, Tom gave his arm to Miss Madeline Bellknap, every Jack did the same to his appointed Jill, and the company filed gayly into the dining-room.

Beginning with the oysters, there was almost a pandemonium of conversation, and tongues wagged fast and eagerly. There were to be no speeches—Tom had determined on that—or rather only a single one, and this was an after-thought. When the champagne was passed, and all the glasses were filled, Tom rose in his seat. Everyone stopped talking, and there was an expectant hush.

" I wish to offer a toast," he said, " a toast for the old bachelors to drink. Wish you merry Christmas and—and here's to *her !* "

There was a brief pause, and then George Hapgood, and in his wake the whole table, rose like one man and emptied their brimming glasses.

" Here's to *her !* "

Tom did not look to right nor to left, not even out of the corner of his eye, as he drained to the last drop the sparkling wine. He would keep to his vow and drink to her in secret. Some of the ladies giggled slightly, and all looked at their plates. It was just a little awkward, even for the most unattached, until Miss Madeline Bellknap rose, glass in hand, and said valiantly, with a wave of her napkin :

" My dears, I give you a toast for you to drink. Wish you merry Christmas. We are old enough to take care of ourselves ; and— and here's to *him !* "

Then there was babel. The women stood up to a woman, and the toast was consummated.

Miss Hardy laughed gayly with the rest. Presently she turned to Tom and said, as if it had suddenly occurred to her, though they had been sitting side by side talking commonplaces ever since dinner began:

"I have not really seen you for years, Mr. Wiggin."

"I have been busy—very busy," said Tom, in a tone which, though he did not intend it to be so, was almost brusque.

"So I have heard. I understand you have been very successful in your business."

"I have stuck to it, that's all."

"I really don't think we have met so as to talk together since Mrs. Carter's ball, and that was—let me see—five years ago this coming New Year's eve. I remember we danced the German together, and—you sent me some flowers which I didn't carry. Perhaps you have forgotten all about it, for five years is a long time and you have been so busy; but I should like to explain to you about those flowers—why I didn't carry them. We are both old enough now to take care of ourselves, so there can't be any objection to my telling you, and—and you won't be offended at this late day, I'm sure. I had several bouquets that night, and Fannie Perkins, who was staying with me, had none. Fannie was shy and sensitive, and it occurred to me to offer one of mine to her. She wouldn't think of it at first, but mother urged her so strongly that she gave in at last. 'Which shall I take, Isabelle?' she asked. I thought a moment and then said, 'Take your pick, Fannie.' And she chose yours. And that is why I didn't carry it to the party. But I think you have forgotten all about it, Mr. Wiggin."

Tom looked as though he had. His chin rested on his collar, and he seemed to be staring at the table-cloth.

"I remember it as if it were yesterday," he said, sadly. "I was a fool."

Miss Hardy colored. "We were both young," she answered, "but now that we are older and wiser, I don't mind admitting on my side that it was stupid of me, to begin with, to give one of my bouquets to anybody, and stupid when I saw that you were put out not to tell you the truth. But wisdom is the reward of years, isn't it?" She talked easily, almost gayly. Tom suddenly realized that he had made a piece of bread which he had been clutching into a sodden ball.

"I'd like to ask you a single question." He was trying to talk easily too. "Why did you let Miss Perkins have her pick? Did you value them all equally?"

"It was because I did not value them all equally that I told her to choose. I did not wish her to think that I cared for one more than the others."

"And whose was that?"

"Five years is a long time, Mr. Wiggin. You said a single question, and this is two. Alas! It is the only point in the story which I have quite forgotten."

"Then why did you tell me?"

"Because I hoped that we might be friends again. When people get to be as old as you and I we value our old friends. There are none exactly like them."

"And that is all?"

"What more is there, Mr. Wiggin? Except to thank you for your lovely book, and to wish you a merry Christmas."

4

"The carriages are waiting," said a servant in Tom's ear.

The dinner was over and it was time to set out for Albion Hall. The ladies filed into the drawing-room, in order, as Miss Madeline phrased it, to give the old bachelors a chance for a short cigar. When that was over Tom bundled his company into carriages, and away they all went in the gayest of spirits.

Whatever belonging to the greenhouse had not been spread over the dinner-table adorned the walls of the dancing-room, and presently as joyous and hilarious a company as anyone would wish to see was tripping to the rhythm of the waltz over a perfect floor. There was just the right number for delightful dancing, no young inexperienced couples to bump into everybody, no things-in-law to stand in the way and look stupid; no one but genuine old stagers taken down from the shelf for one last glorious frolic. You should have seen George Hapgood spinning round with Miss Madeline! How Frazer Bell grinned as he whirled Miss Mamie Scott from one corner of the hall to the other! And Tom? Where was Tom?

QUITE CONTRARY TO THE SPIRIT OF THE OCCASION,
HE WAS DOWN ON HIS KNEES

As some of you who have danced at Albion Hall may remember, there is a very small bower-like ante-room, or off-shoot, or whatever you choose to call it, a sort of adjunct to the supper-room, fit for just one couple to withdraw to. On this Christmas evening it was a veritable hiding-place, for the entrance to it was screened by two noble evergreens which stood as sentinels to demand a password. If the gay company suspected that Tom Wiggin was there, no one was rash enough to peep within and ascertain. Tom Wiggin *was* there, and quite contrary to the spirit of the occasion, he was down on his knees unbosoming the love which he had been smothering for five years to the girl of his heart. Only think of it! And he, a bald-headed old bachelor, and she an old maid old enough to take care of herself. There she sat with her hands before her and a smile on her face, letting him go on. And then, strangest part of all, when he had finished and told how miserable he had been while he was so very busy and absorbed in his business, she suddenly remembered whose bouquet it was she had valued most five years before, although she had declared

an hour earlier that she had totally forgotten.
And then—but the rest is a secret, known
only to the sentinel evergreens and themselves. That is, the rest save one thing. It
was after they had agreed to live as bachelor
and maid no longer, and Tom was sitting
looking at Isabelle as if he had had no dinner, he remarked, with a sudden outburst, as
though he were angry with destiny and a
much outraged being:

"Why on earth did I not find out five
years ago that you loved me?"

"Because," said the pretty spinster in
question, "you never asked me, Tom, dear."

Tom Wiggin looked a trifle sheepish in
spite of his joy. "I never thought of that,"
he said. "I am afraid I never did."

AN EYE FOR AN EYE

AN EYE FOR AN EYE

I

ONE afternoon not many years ago, Henry
Alleyn received word from the hospital of the Sisterhood of St. Vincent de Paul
that Margaret Hogan, an old woman who had
nursed him as a baby, was very sick and desired him to draw her will before she died.
Accordingly he hastened there, taking with
him a young man who was studying law in his
office. It surprised Alleyn that Margaret had
been carried to the hospital, for he had seen
her within a week at her own house where he
was in the habit of paying her occasional visits to relieve her solitude. She had mentioned feeling slightly ill, but, as Alleyn had
heard nothing from her since, he had assumed
that she must be convalescent. He reflected
that she would scarcely have consented to be
removed to the Sisterhood unless she had
been seriously sick, and he felt annoyed that

she had not notified him of her condition, especially as he well knew that her failure to do so proceeded from an absurd reluctance to trouble him, as she called it.

Alleyn was a rising lawyer of about five and thirty, whose conduct of causes had begun to attract attention, which was all the more flattering for the reason that he had come to town but ten years before an unknown youth, without powerful friends to help him on. It was true of him, however, that he was a college graduate, and the possessor of an intelligent face and refined manners which had soon obtained him admission into society. To crown his success, he had within six months become engaged to a charming woman. His future looked bright. He was recognized at the Bar as a man wholly to be trusted.

"I'm afraid that poor Margaret must be on her last legs," he soliloquized as they proceeded. "I'm going," he explained to the student, "to see an old woman who took care of me as a child—a faithful, devoted soul as ever lived. She wants me to make her will. I don't suppose she has much to leave ; though, come to think of it, I believe she owns the little house she lives in free of incumbrances. They have sent me word from the hospital to come at once, so she must be pretty sick, I fear."

"People of that class are apt to imagine themselves at the point of death from very slight cause, are they not?" inquired John Larkin, who, out of respect to his senior, gave an interrogative form to this cynicism.

"Yes, but Margaret is well advanced now, and I have noticed for the last six months that she seemed feeble. I am apprehensive in her case. It was a curious chance," Alleyn continued, "that let me know her whereabouts, some time ago, shortly after I moved here. We had lost track of her for years, as she left my mother's service while I was still a child. It appears she drifted from place to place and finally came to this city to live with a sister. The sister died before very long, and about the same time Margaret chanced to run across my name in the newspaper as counsel in the Brady breach of promise case, which you remember made some stir. With an old woman's faith she assumed that it must be I and looked me up at the office. When she dis-

covered her long lost boy, as she styled me,
she was for throwing her arms around my
neck. She sobbed with delight, and I became the hero of a somewhat embarrassing
spectacle. Faithful old soul! I cannot bear
to think of her suffering."

"It is what we seem to be made for," observed the sententious student.

"But then most of us deserve it. I could
almost vouch that Margaret never did an
evil action in her life," said Alleyn as he
rang at the entrance to the hospital.

Upon mentioning his errand to the servant
who came to the door, Alleyn was shown into
a reception-room, and a few moments later
was informed that he was to go upstairs
to the invalid's chamber. He told Larkin
to remain below until he should send for
him.

"How is Margaret to-night?" he asked of
the girl who showed him the way.

"The doctor thinks she may live a day or
two yet, sir."

On the first landing Alleyn encountered a
pleasant-featured woman in nun's attire who
accorded him a gracious inclination of the
head, in response to which he said :

"I'm the lawyer whom Margaret Hogan sent for."

"Yes, she is expecting you ; her room is up another flight. The Mother is with her."

"Who was that?" he inquired of the servant when they were out of hearing.

"Sister Veronica."

Alleyn was struck by the neatness of everything ; the walls were very white, and as he followed the girl along the passage-way he caught a glimpse through the half-open doors of comfortable looking invalids attended now and again by a Sister of Charity. He reflected that Margaret had acted wisely in being brought there.

"You may go right in, sir," said the girl, pushing open the door of the room at the farther end of the passage-way.

Alleyn entered a moderate-sized chamber. At first he perceived only his old nurse, whose pallid, wrinkled face riveted his attention. Her bed was near the door and she recognized him at once, grasping eagerly the hand which he held out to her with the skinny fingers of both of her own, and exclaiming : "You've come at last. I thought I'd die before you come, Master Henry."

"Nonsense, Margaret, you mustn't talk that way; you'll be better in a day or two."

"No, no, I'll never be any better," answered the old woman in a tone of sad conviction. "I'm wore out. Sit down, Master Henry, the Mother'll give you a chair," she continued, sinking back on the pillows from which she had raised herself a little in her eagerness to greet the young man.

There was a chair a few feet from the bed; while reaching for it Alleyn lifted his eyes and beheld a Sister of Charity standing in the further end of the room with her back to the window. He gave a perceptible start; he could not believe that he saw correctly. "Cora!" he ejaculated below his breath, then made a movement as if to step forward, which was checked by the demeanor of the nun, who, though she had been regarding him since his entrance, gave no sign of recognition save what was conveyed to Alleyn by the faint blush suffusing her countenance; even this was now fading away, betokening that any emotion which his presence had awakened was under her control. As he stood confused and irresolute, she bent her head in a conventional salute, and when their eyes met again there was no vestige of mental agitation on her face. Her complexion had resumed its accustomed marble—a perfect whiteness, rendered all the more striking by the blackness of her hair and superb eyes which rivalled in sombreness her monastic garb. She stood with her hands folded placidly before her, the picture of a tall, commanding, and singularly beautiful woman.

The pause was broken by old Margaret, who, unaware of its significance, and feeling perhaps that every moment was precious to her, craned her head out of bed and quavered: "This is the Mother, Master Henry —I beg your pardon, sir, Mr. Alleyn. She has been very kind to me. Don't go, Mother," she exclaimed piteously, as the nun, again inclining her head, stepped toward the door. "Master Henry won't mind."

"You had better stay," said Alleyn, composedly; "it will distress her if you go, and there is no reason for privacy, I imagine."

At his words the nun, after a moment's hesitation, withdrew again to the further end of the room, where she took a seat by the window. Alleyn, who, though his voice was steady, felt strangely agitated, was glad to be recalled to his professional duty by the voice of the dying woman.

"You'll find everything ready, sir, on that little table."

Following the direction of her gaze, he perceived behind him, close to the wainscoting, the table to which she referred and on which there were writing materials and an accumulation of papers—most of them, as he perceived at a glance, receipted bills. He drew it toward the bed and seated himself. His head was in a whirl, but taking up a pen he said, "You wish me to make your will, Margaret?"

"I want you to fix it so there won't be no trouble after I'm gone."

"I see. To whom do you wish to leave your money?"

"Whom should I be leaving it to but yourself, Master Henry?"

"To me? Nonsense, Margaret; I don't want your money."

"Yes, yes, Master Henry; you and no one else. Who has a better right to it? You as I took care of close on ten year!"

"I'm a thousand times obliged to you, my kind old friend," said Alleyn, tenderly, bending over her, "but I would rather you would make some other disposition of it. You must have relations——"

"No, no," interrupted the sick woman peevishly; "there's not a dollar of it to go to my relations. They never came near me while I was alive. There's no one I care for but you. I said to Mother Eulalie this morning, 'Send for Master Henry and I'll die happy.' I've thought it all out and I know just what I want."

"You will make a much better use of what you have if you leave it in charity—to your Church, for instance," persisted Alleyn.

"No, no," she reiterated; "I want it all to go to you. And, Master Henry," she whispered, confidentially, reaching out her hand and laying it upon Alleyn's, "you'll see there are masses said for me and I'm put in a decent grave? I don't like them tombs. I had the undertaker here this morning and told him all about burying me, so you'll have no trouble."

To draw a will in his own favor was distasteful to Alleyn, but he reflected that the presence of Mother Eulalie, who, from where she was sitting, must be able to hear every word of their conversation, would preclude the possibility of disagreeable charges being brought against him by the next of kin. He was anxious, moreover, to get the matter over as soon as possible, for memories foreign to what he had in hand, and not altogether pleasant, were thronging his brain. He glanced in the direction of the nun; she was staring straight before her at the blank wall, and Alleyn's gaze was fettered a moment by the beauty of her profile. He sighed and turned back his eyes again to the bed, with the compressed lips of one who feels that what, however lamentable, has been done, is done, and that it is useless to deplore.

"Of course, I am bound to obey your wishes in the matter, Margaret," he answered; "if you really desire to leave your property to me, I must draw your will to that effect. Only——"

"That's it, Master Henry."

"Very well," he said, and after a moment's reflection dipped a pen in the ink and began to write. The will was a very simple one and took Alleyn barely ten minutes to draw. By its terms all the estate of Margaret Hogan, of whatever kind, both real and personal, wherever situated and whenever acquired, was given, devised, and bequeathed to Henry Alleyn, his heirs, executors, and administrators, to his and their own use and behoof forever. Said Henry Alleyn was also appointed Executor with the usual powers delegated; that was the whole instrument. When he had finished he told Margaret that he must read it to her, which he did, in a slow, distinct voice so that she might understand every word. While so doing, he glanced for an instant in Mother Eulalie's direction, but it did not seem to him that she was paying attention.

"Is that as you wish it, Margaret?" he inquired at the close.

"Oh, yes, sir, it's beautiful. Now I shall die happy."

Just then the door was pushed open and Sister Veronica appeared. "It's the doctor," she said; "may he come in?"

"Certainly," said Alleyn, "he's the very person I want to see. Will you kindly remain too?" he added to Sister Veronica as he stepped past her to intercept the physician before he should enter. "I shall need you presently."

The interchange of a few words in the passage-way assured Alleyn that Margaret's faculties were entirely unclouded in the estimation of the doctor, who did not hesitate to pronounce her competent to make a will, and who also consented to act as an attesting witness. Alleyn then sent for John Larkin, and while the clerk was coming Margaret was propped up on the pillows by Sister Veronica.

"How long will she live?" whispered Alleyn.

The doctor shrugged his shoulders. "Maybe a week, and she may die to-morrow. It's impossible to say in such cases."

Larkin made his appearance just when the old woman had got on her spectacles. Mother Eulalie was still in the background, and Alleyn chose to remain as indifferent to her presence as she seemed to be to his.

He looked at Sister Veronica and said: "I have asked you to remain to witness this will," then turned and indicating a spot on the paper said: "You will sign here, Margaret."

With infinite pains the old woman feebly scrawled her signature.

"I ain't much of a writer," she observed, squinting ruefully at her handiwork.

"It will do very well," said Alleyn. "Now, Doctor. Margaret," he added, "I understand you to declare this to be your last will and testament."

"Yes, sir," she answered in rather a bewildered fashion. She had fallen back exhausted.

"And it is your wish that these three persons—Dr. Holbrook, Sister Veronica, and my clerk, Mr. Larkin—should sign as attesting witnesses."

"Yes, sir."

The witnesses signed in the order described.

"You should sign your real name, you know," Alleyn remarked to the Sister.

"I know," she said, and wrote "Catharine Sullivan."

"That is all; thank you very much," said Alleyn when the last had finished. The doctor and Sister Veronica immediately took their leave. "I shall not need you any longer," he added to Larkin. "Don't wait for me."

Alleyn sat down beside the bed and began to fold up the will.

"I shall die happy, now," Margaret reiterated.

"You mustn't think of dying; you must think of getting well," he felt prompted to say.

"You'll find everything right," she continued, without heed. "The Mother went to my house yesterday and got the bank-books and things. There's what I've paid out in repairs and groceries since the first," she added, pointing with pride to the pile of bills on the table. "I told the Mother you'd ought to have them. The other things——"

"Yes, yes, Margaret, it'll be time enough by and by," he said, cheerily, getting up and bending over her. "You'll be better to-morrow, and I'll come to see you. I'm afraid of tiring you."

"Good-by, Master Henry, good-by. And you'll remember to have the masses said for me?"

"Never fear, you dear old soul."

He kissed her softly on the forehead, then as he turned to go looked toward the window. Mother Eulalie was sitting with her hands folded before her, still staring at the blank wall. She might have been a statue.

II

Margaret Hogan died that night. A sudden stroke of apoplexy relieved her from further suffering. Alleyn was shocked to hear that she was dead from the undertaker who came to his office on the following morning for instructions. He gave the necessary orders for her interment, and a day or two after his old nurse had been laid in her grave filed the will, which he had drawn, at the Probate Office with a petition to be appointed Executor. Not knowing who were Margaret's next of kin, he published an order of notice, and on the day fixed for the hearing, as no remonstrants appeared, he had no difficulty in obtaining letters of administration from the Court. There was, however, a right of appeal open for thirty days.

Meantime, Alleyn took no steps to reduce the estate into possession, beyond visiting the house and seeing that it was properly closed. He assumed, from what Margaret had said, that her bank-books and any other property belonging to her were in the custody of Mother Eulalie, and for reasons of his own he was in no hurry to revisit the Sisterhood of St. Vincent de Paul.

But after the thirty days had elapsed he felt it incumbent on him to exercise his duties as Executor. It occurred to him that the simplest plan was to send John Larkin to request Mother Eulalie to deliver over the effects of the testatrix. As a matter of caution, however, he told him to stop at the Probate Office on the way, to make sure that no appeal had been entered. Half an hour later the student reappeared with a sardonic grin on his countenance.

"There is one," he said, and produced a paper which he handed to Alleyn.

The lawyer received the copy of the record with a shrug of the shoulders, but after perusing it for a moment knit his brows and observed: "This is confounded impudence. Whom have they retained?"

"Roger K. Harper," responded Larkin, with another grin.

The counsel mentioned was one of the most successful jury lawyers in the community, but a man not over nice in the devices he employed to secure verdicts, and more or less of a demagogue.

The document recited that an appeal was claimed by John Rooney and Ellen Rooney, next of kin, from the decree of the Court allowing a certain instrument offered for probate by Henry Alleyn, wherein said Alleyn was named as Executor, as the last will and testament of Margaret Hogan, deceased. Two of the reasons given, being those ordinarily alleged in probate appeals, were the mental unsoundness of the testatrix and undue influence on the part of said Henry Alleyn; but the third was of more unusual tenor, setting forth that said instrument offered for probate was not the last will and testament of Margaret Hogan, inasmuch as said instrument had been fraudulently altered in the making by said Henry Alleyn.

Alleyn tossed the paper on his desk with a contemptuous air. "It is one of Harper's blood-sucking devices," he said. "He means to bleed me if he can. He has fastened on the wrong man though, as he will find out."

The appeal could not be heard for three months, so Alleyn gave the matter but small heed. So far as desire for the money was concerned, he would willingly have relinquished all claim to it; but he felt bound

to respect Margaret's intention. She had
evidently preferred to cut off her relatives,
and Alleyn argued that it would hardly
be respectful if he should vacate his rights
merely to dispose of a disagreeable suit which
was absolutely groundless. Until the appeal
should be tried his powers as Executor were
suspended. Accordingly he addressed a formal letter to the Sisterhood of St. Vincent de
Paul, to the effect that as certain complications had arisen in relation to the affairs of
the late Margaret Hogan, her Executor would
await their settlement before taking possession of the property of the deceased. To
this communication Alleyn received no answer.

As time wore on he was rather surprised
at hearing nothing from the other side. He
fully expected to be approached with a view
to a compromise, and had been looking forward to the amusement he should derive
from disappointing his pettifogging opponent. To make the first advances himself
would be clearly an admission of weakness.
Besides, he was resolved not to pay a dollar.
When a week before the day of trial he had
still heard nothing he put his case into the

hands of Charles Davenant, an intimate friend and brother lawyer of repute, who was some years his senior.

"It's a fishing excursion, I take it," said Mr. Davenant, when Alleyn had finished his recital.

"I had supposed so, certainly. But I'm at a loss to understand why Harper has not been near me. There must be some cat in the meal, I am beginning to think, though I can't imagine what. Dr. Holbrook will testify as to Margaret's mental condition, and as to undue influence there isn't a shadow of evidence. The only time she ever spoke to me about her will was the day she made it."

"How about the third reason?" asked Mr. Davenant. "It is so unusual that I should judge they expected to make something out of it."

"It is insulting enough, I admit; but what have they got to substantiate it?" said Alleyn, with some irritation.

"You say that while you were drawing the will there was no one in the room except this Mother Eulalie?"

"Yes."

"What sort of a looking woman was she?"

" A young woman—a very handsome woman," said Alleyn, with slow emphasis.

" Could she have heard your client's conversation ? "

" She could have heard it, unquestionably, but I doubt very much if she did. I looked at her several times, and on each occasion she seemed to me not to be paying the slightest attention to what was going on. She was sitting close to the window some twenty-five feet away. You see I have considered the situation. But what if she did hear us ? " he added, with a nervous laugh.

" Have you been to see her ? " asked Mr. Davenant.

" No. I—er—I thought it better not. Don't you think it would be compromising ? "

The senior shrugged his shoulders. " I appreciate your point, of course, but I do not regard it as of much moment. By so doing you could relieve your uncertainty and ascertain whether or not to summon her as a witness. If her testimony corroborates yours, there's an end of the whole business. If, on the other hand, it fails to do so, you will not be caught unprepared."

“How can her testimony fail to corroborate mine?” Alleyn asked, with another touch of indignation.

“Ah, my dear fellow, there you ask conundrums. Forewarned is forearmed, that’s all. If there is anything in the case beyond mere bluff, I am inclined to believe that it must be in connection with this Mother Eulalie, as you call her. She may have looked wise or dropped dark hints which these ignorant people have repeated to brother Harper. When you have been in practice as long as I have you will appeciate that you can never be sure what anyone will testify — especially a woman.”

Alleyn frowned and looked annoyed.

“I understood you to state that you asked the testatrix if she didn’t wish to leave something to the Church,” continued Mr. Davenant.

“Yes; and she said distinctly that she did not.”

“Precisely. Supposing Mother Eulalie testifies that she heard differently?”

“It would be a falsehood,” protested Alleyn, with a warmth that amused the older lawyer.

"The jury would have to pass upon that," was the dry comment.

Alleyn drummed on the table reflectively for a few moments. "I don't care to go to see her," he said, at length. "I'll take the chance," he added, with an effort at nonchalance.

"Ninety-nine chances out of a hundred you will be just as well off," said Mr. Davenant.

A few days later Alleyn read in one of the morning papers the following statement: "Among the causes set down for trial at the current term of the Supreme Court is Henry Alleyn, Executor, v. John Rooney and Ellen Rooney, appellants; an appeal from the finding of the Probate Court of this County, allowing the will of one Margaret Hogan, who died during the last six months, leaving an estate valued at thirty thousand dollars, all of which by the terms of the will was bequeathed to Henry Alleyn, a lawyer of this city. The next of kin, first cousins of the testatrix, allege in their petition insanity, undue influence, and fraudulent alteration of the contents of the will by Mr. Alleyn, who appears to have drawn the instrument in question. Hon. Roger K. Harper has been retained to represent the interests of the appellants, and it is reported that there will be peculiar and startling developments at the trial."

"Thirty thousand dollars! Bah!" said Alleyn to himself after the disagreeable smart occasioned by seeing his name in print in such a connection had subsided. "Though, to tell the truth, I don't know what she left. The house is worth six thousand. This business has taught me one lesson: never to draw a will in my own favor again. Pshaw!" he added, reflectively. "Even if Cora wishes to do me an injury, what can she say?"

On the morning of the day fixed for the trial Alleyn came into the court-room with a deliberately cheery air. Counsel were already in their places and there was a considerable number of lookers on. He glanced at once toward the benches reserved for witnesses and recognized only Dr. Holbrook, whom he had summoned to be present. Just then the attention of every one was attracted by the unaccustomed entrance of two Sisters of Charity, the first of whom, as she walked behind the usher to a seat, he perceived to be

Mother Eulalie; the other was Sister Veronica. Her he had been obliged to send for as a witness. But why had Mother Eulalie come? Possibly as a companion. So at least Alleyn tried to persuade himself as he sat down beside his counsel. The appearance of the nuns was evidently matter for conjecture, to judge from the wagging and craning of heads. The court-room seemed to have become animated. Alleyn did not choose to look again, but Mr. Davenant turned his head with the rest.

"Is that she?" he said in a whisper, nudging Alleyn.

"Yes."

"The handsome one?"

"Yes."

"She's an extraordinarily beautiful woman."

The entrance of the Court, at which everybody rose, put an end to their dialogue.

"What is the first case on the list, Mr. Clerk?" asked the Judge.

"Henry Alleyn, Executor, *v.* John Rooney and Ellen Rooney, appellants."

"Are both parties ready?"

The Counsel signified that they were, and after the jury had been impanelled, Mr. Davenant, upon whom it was incumbent to take the initiative so far as to prove the will over again, called his witnesses to be sworn. They were the three attesting witnesses to the will. He first put Dr. Holbrook on the stand, who acknowledged his own signature, declared that he had seen the testatrix sign the will, and in answer to a series of carefully framed questions stated that he had attended Margaret Hogan from the time she entered the hospital until her death, that her intelligence was unclouded during that period, and that he regarded her as entirely qualified, so far as her mental condition was concerned, to dispose of her property.

"He is your witness," said Mr. Davenant to his opponent.

"I understand you, Doctor, that you consider the testatrix to have been of thoroughly sound mind at the time of the execution of this instrument?" said Roger Harper, slowly.

"I do, sir."

"I think you said, Doctor, that though her bodily condition was enfeebled, her intellect was to all intents and purposes unaffected— that, in short, she knew perfectly well what she was about?"

"I did, sir," answered Dr. Holbrook in a decided tone, which showed that he was little in sympathy with his questioner.

"Precisely," said the lawyer. He looked around the court-room with an air of triumph, as though the testimony of the witness was exactly to his liking.

"One more question, Doctor. Were you present while this will was being drawn?"

"I was not."

"Am I not right in saying that you saw or knew nothing of the making of this will beyond the fact that the testatrix signed it in your presence?"

"That is all I know, sir."

"Precisely. That will do, Doctor."

John Larkin was the next witness. He testified to having seen the testatrix sign her name. Upon cross-examination Roger Harper asked him but one question—the same which he had put to the doctor—"Were you present while this will was being drawn?"

"I was present after it had been drawn," replied the student, sophistically.

"I did not ask you whether you were present after it had been drawn, Mr. Larkin.

You will please answer my question. Were
— you — present — while—this—will—was—
being—drawn?"

"No, sir."

"That is all, Mr. Larkin."

"They evidently mean to base their case
on the charge of fraudulent alteration,"
whispered Mr. Davenant to Alleyn, as he
summoned Catharine Sullivan, *alias* Sister
Veronica, to the stand.

The pleasant-featured nun seemed bewildered, and testified in an unintelligent way to
her own signature, and to having seen Margaret Hogan sign.

"Were you present while the will was being drawn, Sister Veronica?" asked Roger
Harper, when his turn to cross-examine
came.

"No, sir, I knew nothing about it whatever," answered the witness with a promptitude that caused Mr. Davenant to mutter to
Alleyn : "They've fixed her, that's evident."

"That's all, Sister Veronica," said Roger
Harper.

Mr. Davenant then claimed that his client
had established a *prima facie* case, to which
his Honor assented.

G

"I am ready to hear your evidence, Mr. Harper," said the Judge.

Roger Harper rose slowly and came forward. He was a large man, in the prime of middle life, with a prominent hawk's nose, deep-set, lustrous eyes, and a smooth-shaven, forcible upper lip. His iron-gray hair fell low on his forehead, and almost mingled with his bushy brows.

"May it please the Court," he began; "Mr. Foreman and gentlemen of the jury, in the course of a long professional experience—and mine has been an active experience of thirty years—I have never been called upon to present evidence so remarkable in its character as that which it has become my painful duty to lay before you. Far be it from me to to desire the ruin of any brother in that profession of which I am proud to call myself a member—a profession whose prosperity is founded upon the trust which the great public, to which you, gentlemen, belong, repose in the integrity, uprightness, and honor of those who constitute it. But, gentlemen, worthy of implicit belief as I hold the word of a lawyer to be, it is for you to say whether it is not outweighed in the scale of verity by the evidence of one who comes in the sacred vestments of religion to confront yea with nay. I shall produce in this case, gentlemen of the jury, but one witness. But through the testimony of that one witness I expect to overthrow this will offered for probate, by proving that its contents were fraudulently altered by Henry Alleyn, the Executor therein named and a member of this Bar. It is the saddest duty which I have ever had to perform. If you find a verdict in my favor it will mean professional disgrace and downfall for him whom I have mentioned; but if you find that Margaret Hogan executed her will in this man's favor, meaning so to do—and, gentlemen, the doctor has told you she was in her right mind—you will have to declare that Mother Eulalie, the Superior of the Sisterhood of St. Vincent de Paul, has been guilty of the blackest perjury."

He paused, and one could have heard a pin drop in the court-room. Those who knew Alleyn glanced at him. He sat with folded arms smiling contemptuously, but Mr. Davenant looked rather grave.

"Mother Eulalie, you will come forward and be sworn," said Roger Harper.

Amid profound stillness the nun passed up the aisle to where the clerk was standing ready to administer the oath. Her beauty was absorbing. Men were at a loss, perhaps, to understand how it happened that curves so full of symmetry, and eyes so lustrous, should be shrouded by the apparel of the cloister. Save for the pallor of her complexion there was almost a suggestion of fleshliness in the luscious contour of face and figure, but, after the first glance, those gazing fancied that they saw the devout servant of God who, branded by the iron of mortal woe, has sought refuge on the bosom of the Church. She might well be a saint because she had been a sinner; and yet no demure, bloodless embodiment of sanctity, but vital still with the human forces of energy and passion. Even the crucifix upon her breast seemed to rise and fall with the undulations of a breast through which the tide of life flowed far from sluggishly. She was one of whom the Church might have been proud in the days when the mandates of its functionaries wrested sceptres from the grasp of kings. So the spectators thought of her as she stood with uplifted hand in obedience to the bidding of the clerk.

"You do solemnly swear that in the cause now in hearing you will speak the truth, the whole truth, and nothing but the truth, so help you God."

"I do, so help me God," she murmured, and she looked, as it appeared to Alleyn, straight at him.

"What is your full name?" asked Roger Harper.

"Cora Lloyd Dennison."

"And your occupation?"

"I am the Mother Superior of the Sisterhood of St. Vincent de Paul in this city."

"Where you are known as Mother Eulalie, I believe?"

"Yes."

"How long have you been the Mother Superior of the Sisterhood?"

"Five years. I came there twelve years ago, but was a Sister during seven years."

"Now, Mother Eulalie, I should like you to tell the jury in your own words exactly what you know, if you know anything, in regard to the making of the alleged will of Margaret Hogan on the fifth day of November last past."

"I was sitting in the sick woman's room

about five o'clock in the afternoon of that day," she began slowly, "when a gentleman entered—a lawyer, who said that he had come to make her will. She was expecting him, for she had told me to send for him early in the day, as she thought she was going to die."

" Do you remember the gentleman's name?"

"I do. Henry Alleyn."

" Do you see him here? "

"I do. He is sitting right in front of me."

"Go on."

" There was no one in the room except us three. He sat down beside the bed at a table. I was sitting by the window at the further end of the room."

" At what distance were you from the bed ? "

" About twenty-five feet. They both spoke in rather a low tone, but I could hear perfectly the conversation. He said, 'Margaret, whom do you wish to leave your money to ? ' ' Master Henry,' she said, ' I want it to go to the Church, every dollar of it.' "

" Go on."

" ' Have you no relations ? ' " he asked. ' I don't want it to go to my relations, Master Henry, I want the Church to have it.' ' Very well ; you must tell me what churches,' he answered. 'The Church of the Redeemer and the Chapel of the Holy Virgin ; each half. You'll know how to do it.' 'I understand, Margaret. There should be an Executor appointed, though.' 'Couldn't you be the Executor, Master Henry ? ' 'If you wish me to.' 'You fix it so,' she said. After that he began to write. When he had finished he read it to her and the contents ran exactly as the will which is offered as the true will, excepting that all the property was left to be divided between the two churches instead of to Mr. Alleyn. Then the others came in and she signed the will."

There was a death-like stillness in the court. Again every one looked at Alleyn. He had flushed violently at her convicting words, and was bending forward staring at her with an expression that was half terror, half bewilderment. Charles Davenant, too, was watching her with keen scrutiny. Her marvellous story had been told simply and without effort. There had been no hesitation, no embarrassment. Only the grimness of it made men who knew Henry Alleyn reflect that it could not be true.

"You say that the conversation between the testatrix and Mr. Alleyn was in rather a low tone," continued Roger Harper, after there had been a pause sufficient to allow the evidence to impress the minds of the jury. "Can you give any idea of how low?"

"About as low as I am speaking now," she said, sinking her voice a very little. "But not a single word escaped me. I listened at first inadvertently, then because I happened to notice Mr. Alleyn glance at me once or twice as though to ascertain if I were listening. I heard everything."

"What became of the will after it was signed?"

"Mr. Alleyn took it away with him."

"Whether or not the testatrix ever took the will into her own hands and read it?"

"She never did."

"Is there any other evidence that you can give which will throw light upon this matter, Mother Eulalie?"

"I have these," she said, producing a number of bank-books. "Margaret Hogan sent me to her house for them the day before she died. 'They're to go to the Church,' she sa——"

"I object, your Honor," interrupted Mr. Davenant.

"There is a question here, your Honor," replied Roger Harper, "as to whether or not the testatrix wished to dispose of her property according to the terms of this will offered by my brother. It seems to me that contemporaneous declarations of the testatrix are admissible to show fraud on the part of the person who drew the will."

The Judge reflected a moment. "I shall admit the evidence," he said, finally. "You may continue," he added, to the witness.

"'They're to go to the Church,' she said; 'I want you to take care of them.'"

"What is the amount of money which these books represent?" asked Roger Harper.

"Between twenty-four and twenty-five thousand dollars."

"There is only one remaining question that I wish to put to you, Mother Eulalie. State whether or not you had ever seen or known Henry Alleyn before you saw him on the day when this will was drawn?"

The nun deliberately fixed her brilliant eyes on the young man, and they seemed to

him to wear an expression of triumph as she
said, firmly, "I had never seen him or heard
of him in my life."

Alleyn, who was awaiting her response
with impatience, threw himself back in his
chair aghast. "Ask her"—he whispered
feverishly, bending toward his counsel ; then
he stopped and fell back again. "It's a lie,"
he muttered so that many heard him.

"She is your witness," said Roger Harper.

The cross-examination of a beautiful woman is at best no easy matter. Charles Davenant put his questions with admirable skill,
but failed to catch Mother Eulalie tripping
in a single particular. He made her re-
hearse in detail everything that took place
from the moment that Alleyn entered the
sick-room until he left it, but her story coin-
cided precisely with what she had already
stated, and disclosed no inconsistencies. Not
once did she lose her head or appear flurried,
but that she was laboring under deep excitement was evident to those who watched the
pallor of her face change gradually to rose as
she parried thrust after thrust of the skilful
lawyer. But who would not betray agitation under a similar ordeal ? The fact that

she did so could not fairly be a cause for suspicion ; while, on the other hand, her distress, especially as her comeliness was enhanced thereby, could not fail to work upon the minds of the jury.

Mr. Davenant purposely prolonged the examination until the noon recess so that he might have an opportunity to go on with it after having had an interview with his client. He hurried Alleyn to a private room in a hotel, where he ordered lunch.

"There is some mystery here that you can clear up, my dear fellow," he said, laying his hand on Alleyn's knee.

"The woman is lying."

"Granted ; but a woman does not lie for nothing."

"I know of no explanation," replied Alleyn, curtly.

Mr. Davenant was puzzled. He had not seriously supposed that his client would be able to elucidate the case, but he had put the question to him in desperation. He was now forced back on a previous presumption, that she was lying for the sake of the Church. But the difficulty was, as he proceeded to note to Alleyn, that the Church would be no

better off if the will were upset. The next
of kin would be entitled to the money, unless,
indeed, Roger Harper should have conceived
the idea of subsequently setting up the alleged suppressed will from the lips of his
lovely witness. But such a scheme was a
rash hazard, to say the least, involving nice
legal difficulties. Altogether, it was the
strangest affair with which he had ever been
connected.

"Is there nothing you think of which I
can ask her that will help us?" he inquired
almost imploringly.

"Nothing. It is simply my word against
hers. Great God! Davenant, this means
ruin for me!" Alleyn rose and began to pace
the room feverishly.

"Not so bad as that."

"Yes, ruin! 'What motive had she for
lying?' every one will ask. 'Alleyn drew the
will himself in his own favor and supposed
the nun was not listening. One more good
man gone wrong;' that's what the world will
say."

"It was a very stupid device, then. A
clever man like you would hardly put his
head into such a noose."

"The world does not make such subtile distinctions. Davenant, have I deserved this? It is horrible! horrible!"

Alleyn fell into a chair and covered his face with his hands. It occurred to his friend, who was eating raw oysters with deliberation, whether by any possibility there might be truth in the accusation after all. The suspicion was too dreadful to entertain, but it haunted him. He did his best to cheer Alleyn, begging him to remember that the fight was only half over and that it behooved him to keep up his courage to the end; very likely the jury would disagree, and before the case could be tried again a compromise might be arranged, or evidence might be forthcoming regarding Mother Eulalie that would give it a different aspect.

As they went back, the newsboys were calling out, "Two o'clock edition; startling developments in the Hogan will case," and Alleyn read in large letters on one of the bulletin boards, "A serious charge. Testimony in the Hogan will case affecting the character of lawyer Henry Alleyn of this city. He is accused of fraudulently altering the will of Margaret Hogan for his own bene-

fit." He quivered in every vein at the sounds
and sight. The news had travelled fast, for
the court-room was crowded. There were
many faces he recognized. The members of
the Bar had been drawn thither by the unusual character of the evidence, and all eyes
were bent on him curiously as he walked to
his seat, doing his best not to appear disconcerted.

Mr. Davenant continued his cross-examination for another half-hour, inquiring as to
the witness's past life, so far as the Judge
would allow; but he elicited nothing of moment.

"That is my whole case," said his opponent, when the nun had left the stand.

Alleyn was called in rebuttal. His direct
testimony took the remainder of the day. It
was clear and unequivocal. He repeated the
exact conversation that had taken place between him and Margaret, and described every
circumstance of their interview with great
minuteness under the searching examination
of Mr. Davenant. His manner was spiritless,
however; he seemed dejected, almost broken,
which was not adapted to produce a favorable impression on those listening to him

On the following morning he was taken in hand by Roger Harper, who badgered and finally angered him by the style of his cross-examination; as, for instance, by jeering at the idea that he had not been aware of the amount of his old nurse's property, and by insidiously referring to his approaching marriage and consequent need of money. Alleyn flushed with indignation and lost his head. His answers to the questions put to him became sarcastic and sophistical.

After he had been dismissed there was no more evidence to offer, and Roger Harper began his closing address to the jury, in the presence of a densely packed court-room.

"Gentlemen," he said in the course of his argument, "my learned brother who is to follow me in the presentation of this case will undoubtedly ask you if it could be that a young man of hitherto spotless reputation, with a brilliant future in prospect and with everything to lose in the event of his being detected, would be stupid enough—would be wilfully blind enough, to fraudulently alter a last will and testament in the manner which has been described to you by my witness— would be blind enough, I repeat, to do this in the presence of a third person within easy ear-shot of whom he was obliged to read aloud the contents of an instrument different from that which he now offers for probate? Why did he not send the witness out of the room, my brother will ask? Why did he not adopt one of a thousand artifices that could have been thought of to screen himself from exposure? The element of extreme improbability is so prominent, that one is prompted to cry out, 'Such a thing would be impossible.' So it seems, certainly, when you consider the facts thus barely stated. But, gentlemen of the jury, let me ask you this: Which is the more improbable, that this young man would have acted in the manner indicated, or that a woman—she whose testimony you have listened to—would deliberately commit perjury to ruin forever one whom she never saw or heard of? There can be but one answer to my question. You must decide in her favor, unless you can perceive some motive why she should offer false testimony — she, a priestess of God, and given up to the thoughts and offices of religion. Where is the motive? Her statement that they had never met before is not denied.

How could she be benefited by swearing falsely? If this will falls to the ground, the next of kin and not the churches will get the money. Remember that, gentlemen of the jury. Remember, too, that this young man, this rising young attorney, was shortly to have been married; and you can all imagine, in view of so interesting a circumstance, that thirty thousand dollars would have been a most welcome addition to his resources. Gentlemen, I repeat it, where is the motive?"

Roger Harper spoke but half an hour. Mr. Davenant then rose. Although he had been forestalled in his argument of want of probability, he pressed it cogently, dwelling on the good repute of Alleyn and the terrible consequences of an ill-considered verdict as affecting his client's future career. It was true, he said, that there seemed a lack of motive on the part of the Mother Superior, but even if it be admitted that there could have been no adequate reason why she should swear falsely, was it not much more rational to suppose that she had been mistaken in what she heard, than that this lawyer of well-known integrity had committed so heinous a fault?

7

Her testimony was that she had heard the old woman give him certain directions which were carried out in the will which he read. Therefore he must have deliberately falsified the instrument while drawing it. The alteration must, of course, have been made on the spot, for there was not an erasure. Such a cold-blooded, deliberate piece of villany was out of the question.

Mr. Davenant's harangue was able and to the point, but somehow it lacked fervor, as though the advocate were unable to explain to himself, satisfactorily, the discrepancy in the evidence. Moreover, Alleyn's attitude during its delivery was scarcely adapted to encourage his counsel. He sat looking gloomy and downcast, with the demeanor of one who expects the worst.

The Judge's charge was short and impartial. He adverted to the fact that the accusation made was of a most serious character, involving the good repute of the plaintiff, and that the jury ought to weigh the evidence offered on both sides with the greatest deliberation ; but that while so doing they must not allow themselves to be influenced by emotional considerations of any kind. The questions for them to decide were simply these, he said:

1. Was the testatrix of sound mind when she executed the will?

2. Was the testatrix acting under the undue influence of Henry Alleyn at the time of executing said will?

3. Was the instrument offered for probate executed as the last will and testament of Margaret Hogan?

As regards the first two, there could be no doubt as to what their verdict must be, for no evidence had been offered by the appellants either of lack of mental capacity or of undue influence. The whole contest was regarding the third reason, and as to this there was nothing he could say that would help them. The burden of proof was on those offering the will for probate, to show by a preponderance of the evidence that it had been duly executed; but the term preponderance of evidence did not necessarily mean numerical preponderance; the quality rather than the quantity should be taken into consideration. They had listened to the testimony and must make up their minds as to whom to believe, taking into due account the liability of human beings to error as to what is seen and heard.

It was late in the afternoon when the jury retired, so that no verdict could be rendered until the next day.   Alleyn thanked Mr. Davenant in a perfunctory, dazed sort of manner for his services and left the court.

"What do you make of the case, Davenant?" asked a white-haired member of the Bar, drawing him aside. "It seems to me very extraordinary."

"Frankly, sir, I don't know what to make of it.   It is the most inexplicable affair which I have ever had to deal with.   I'm all at sea."

The intervening hours were terrible for Alleyn.   He could not sleep.   The newspapers had enormous head-lines and full details relating to the trial, set off by pen portraits of the principal personages implicated. The city was all agog with the excruciating scandal, and the court-room on the following morning was packed to overflowing.   It had been whispered abroad that the jury had agreed and would be in their places.

"Gentlemen of the jury," said the Clerk, "do you find that Margaret Hogan at the time she executed the instrument alleged to be her last will and testament was of sound mind?"

"To that interrogatory, the jury's answer is 'Yes,'" said the foreman.

"Do you find that Margaret Hogan at the time she executed said instrument was acting under undue influence?"

"To that interrogatory the jury's answer is 'No.'"

"Do you find that said instrument was duly executed by said Margaret Hogan as her last will and testament?"

"To that interrogatory the jury's answer is 'No,' for the reason that said instrument was fraudulently altered by Henry Alleyn, the Executor named therein."

From that verdict there was no appeal.

III

ONE evening about five years later, Charles Davenant was standing in his drawing-room with his back to the fire, awaiting the arrival of some friends whom he had asked to dinner. Time had given him the portly appearance which befits the successful, well-to-do lawyer. He was to-day one of the recognized leaders of the Bar, the counsel for rich corporations and trustee of large estates. The guests expected by him were the members of a locally celebrated law club to which he belonged.

The first to appear was the white-haired Nestor who had questioned him at the conclusion of the Hogan will case. He was still hale, but betrayed by a hesitating gait, as he came into the room, the limitations of fourscore.

"Good-evening, Mr. Perkins, you as ever lead all, I see," said his host advancing to greet the veteran. "I am very glad to see you, Harper," Mr. Davenant added to another guest who followed close behind. "I do not need to introduce you two, gentlemen."

"He must have a long spoon who would eat with the devil," observed John Larkin to an associate with whom he had just reached the landing as they caught sight of the somewhat anomalous tableau presented by the conversative Mr. Perkins and Roger K. Harper cordially shaking hands.

"Nothing succeeds like success," was the

answer, and a moment later both the speaker and his sardonically inclined companion were imitating the example set them by their distinguished senior.

Roger K. Harper was the only one of the fifteen lawyers composing Mr. Davenant's dinner company who was not a member of the club, and, as the guests arrived, others, doubtless, wondered a little why it had occurred to their host to invite him. But however fastidious they could afford to be at heart, no one saw fit to be otherwise than cordial to the formidable advocate whose long list of victories before a jury had won for him a vast clientage. His contemporaries dated the real founding of his fortunes from the now famous probate appeal which had wrought the ruin of Henry Alleyn. He had been successful before, but the verdict in that cause had placed him upon a pinnacle from which neither justice nor envy could dislodge him.

After the party was seated at table the conversation became almost immediately animated and brilliant. There was everything to inspire wit and anecdote; the surroundings were artistic yet cosey, the service exemplary, the viands delicious. The first glass of wine was an assurance that their host had not spared his cellar. Each bit of humor, each graphic experience reminded some one of another, and so the ball was kept rolling. Mr. Davenant himself seemed in the best of spirits. On his right sat Roger Harper, and on his left, as it happened, the Justice who had presided at the well-known trial. At the opposite end of the table John Larkin officiated. He was in active practice now, and doing extremely well. To him had fallen the task of winding up his former patron's affairs, and he had managed to retain as clients a majority of those accustomed to do business with Alleyn.

Although the proximity at table of three of the chief actors in the still remembered drama must have struck as an odd coincidence most of those present, every one to whom the idea of calling attention to it occurred was restrained by the peculiar nature of the case, the mystery surrounding which had never been cleared away. Within a fortnight after the verdict Henry Alleyn had left town, without, so far as was known, making any effort to re-establish his damaged reputation, and since then nothing had been heard of him beyond the vague report that he was living in Europe. There had been at the time some talk of having him disbarred, but the fact that this suggestion had never taken the form of a petition for the purpose to the Court was evidence that the lawyers in the community were not fully satisfied that Mother Eulalie's testimony was unimpeachable. What had added to their reluctance to take final action was, doubtless, an item which had appeared in the newspapers not more than a month after the trial, to the effect that the Mother Superior had resigned her position at the Sisterhood of St. Vincent de Paul and had also left the city. Nervous exhaustion resulting from the painful ordeal which she had undergone was popularly ascribed as the cause, but all the same there were those among the members of the Bar who shrugged their shoulders as they read the paragraph.

After some remarkably fine Burgundy had been served and the cigars were lighted a hush fell upon the company as each one settled himself luxuriously in his chair, rather disposed in the fulness of his content to listen to the wit of others, than to make fresh sallies of his own. The pause thus afforded was broken by the Judge, who observed, in somewhat a judicial tone, "A wonderful glass of wine."

"Wonderful," some one repeated in echo of this voice of authority.

"It is some which poor Henry Alleyn sent me only a few weeks before his misfortune," said Mr. Davenant.

"Indeed," said his Honor, "indeed; I applaud his taste. A very remarkable case, that," he added, reflectively. "I haven't to this day been satisfied in my own mind as to which of them spoke the truth. Eh, brother Harper?"

Deep silence followed this appeal and all eyes were bent eagerly on the eloquent advocate, who pursed his lips and puffed at his cigar a moment before replying—a mannerism, and one apt to be imitated by those who reasonably expect their words to be counted on to be weighty, but in this particular instance effective.

"Your Honor, it is my belief that the woman was lying," he said, laconically.

Every one waited for him to go on.

"But, on the other hand," he continued slowly, "I have no more real knowledge on the subject than any one of you. She came to me with the story exactly as you heard it at the trial. She was already aware that the Church could not take the money, and when I asked her if she had any acquaintance with Alleyn, her answer was, as subsequently, 'I have never seen or heard of him in my life.' It is my private belief that this last statement was false. If so, the whole was false. But I have not a shred of evidence to offer in support of my assertion. It is mere conjecture."

"What has become of Alleyn?" asked one of the company presently.

"At last accounts he was in Paris—a wanderer upon the face of the earth," responded John Larkin.

"He is dead," quietly interjected Mr. Davenant.

"Dead? You don't say so!" exclaimed several.

"Yes, he was mortally wounded in August last, fighting on the Prussian side against the French. I have here a communication received ten days ago from the German in command of his regiment, which I will read you presently. But first let me throw some light on the matter of which you were just speaking. On the day before Alleyn went away," continued Mr. Davenant, producing a packet which he laid upon the table, "he came to see me. I had tried in vain numberless times already to induce him to admit that there was a mystery, but he had always shaken his head and declared that he had nothing to say. I saw from his face that it would be useless to ask questions, but I could not help exclaiming: 'Alleyn, you are going abroad forever, you say; do not, for God's sake, let this horrible accusation stain men's memory of you if it is possible for you to clear it away.' He looked me in the eyes —I shall remember the sadness of his expression so long as I live—and shook his head. 'Davenant,' he said, 'whatever it is desirable to have explained will be explained some day. Good-by.' He kept his word. The Prussian officer's letter contained another, sealed and addressed to me and superscribed, 'To be delivered only in case of my death.' It contains the clew to the mystery, at least the only clew I have," he added, opening the packet. "Listen. This is dated a week after the trial. 'Henry, your life is ruined forever, and I have done it. Do you know why? Do you remember what you wrote me thirteen years ago? "God knows I love you, darling, but what is this all to lead to? You must realize that I cannot marry you. I have my way to make in the world." That was all, and you were free—free to hold your head erect and live respected and happy. How did it fare with me? Has it ever occurred to you, Henry? As with so many others, the world spat upon me. I became a vile, shameless thing—such as you are now. I could not hold up my head. What had I done more than you? Why should I be the only one to suffer? They called me a dishonest woman. I began to ask myself what is a dishonest man? You know the feelings of one now, and you know how I felt. You are suffering as I was made to suffer. You need not blame me, Henry. Blame the world.

"'CORA.'"

"Mother Eulalie!"

"Is it possible?"

"Horrible!"

Such was the variety of ejaculations uttered around the table when Mr. Davenant finished.

"I see—I see," murmured Roger Harper in a hoarse whisper at their close. "Marvellous—marvellous."

The jury advocate's face was luminous. The cobwebs of mystification had been swept away in an instant and the truth lay bare before him. But used as he was to astounding revelations, and freely as he had predicated that there was falsehood here, it was evident from his expression that he was moved to wonder. "Allow me, Mr. Davenant," he said, "to look at that letter."

He scanned it admiringly, while the company eyed him in silence. "I can see it all now. Marvellous—marvellous!" he reiterated. "'They called me a dishonest woman. I began to ask myself what is a dishonest man? You know the feelings of one now, and you know how I felt.' There is real tragedy for you, gentlemen. No make-believe stage business."

"It was revenge, cruel, relentless revenge," said Mr. Perkins.

"Yes, it was revenge," retorted Roger Harper slowly, compressing the bowl of his

Burgundy glass with so strenuous a grip that it might well have been crushed to fragments. "Cruel, relentless revenge, if you will. But was it not justice, too? Think a moment, gentlemen. She loved him and he left her. What ways does the world provide for making man share in—for making man even understand the misery which an erring woman undergoes? Why should she be the only one to suffer? She asks the question. Can you answer it?"

His penetrating gaze swept round the circle, but not a voice replied to his inquiry. The lawyers seemed to be musing.

"An eye for an eye, a tooth for a tooth, a life for a life," said John Larkin, with sententious emphasis.

"Why did not Alleyn publish that letter to the world?" asked some one.

"For the same reason that he did not contradict Mother Eulalie's testimony at the trial that she had never seen or heard of him before—a guilty conscience," responded Roger Harper, keenly. "She knew that he would not contradict her, and she knew that he would not disclose the contents of that letter so long as he lived. There was woman's genius! They were master-strokes," he added with professional enthusiasm.

"It is a strange, sad story," said the Judge, breaking in upon another silence. "Heinous as was the woman's crime, I cannot help agreeing with my brother opposite that there was a certain poetic justice in the consequences. While the code of society continues to make subtile distinctions between almost equally guilty parties, one can scarcely be surprised that those who suffer under its operation should sometimes disregard all law in their efforts to obtain justice. As one having authority I am shocked, but as a human being I feel reflective."

"There is force undoubtedly in your Honor's suggestion," said Mr. Perkins; "but admitting the justice of the consequences here, I find it difficult to forget that if humanity is to look for mercy and forgiveness anywhere it must be to woman. Could this Mother Eulalie really have loved Alleyn and have acted as she did?"

"One moment, Mr. Perkins, if you please," exclaimed Davenant. "I should have read you the Prussian commander's letter. This is a translated copy.

"' Mr. Charles Davenant—

"' Sir : It has become my melancholy duty to inform you that Henry Alleyn, an American, serving as a private soldier under my command, was shot through the lungs at the battle of Gravelotte, and died from the effects of his wound four days later. He had on several occasions attracted attention by his conspicuous gallantry, and would, but for his untimely death, have received the promotion he deserved. At his own request his body has been buried in German soil. He desired that I should inform you of his decease, and forward you the enclosed packet. He was conscious to the last, and was tenderly nursed by a very handsome lady, also an American, in the garb of a Sister of Charity, whose name I have been unable to obtain, and who disappeared on the day after he was laid to rest. Condoling with you in your bereavement, I remain, with high respect and esteem,

"' Your very obedient servant,

"' Kleinmann, Colonel.'"

"Your doubt is answered," said Roger Harper, impressively, to Mr. Perkins.

8

The old man bowed. "So she was with him at the last. Poor devil," he said.

"To which of them do you refer, sir?" inquired John Larkin.

"You are right, young man. Poor devils, then."

"With all my heart."

There was another hush. The lawyers were musing again.

"This is extraordinarily fine wine, upon my soul, Davenant," said his Honor at length, as the outcome of his cogitations.

IN FLY-TIME

IN FLY-TIME

TOM NICHOLS, the architect, lay back in his hammock with a contented air. He was comfortable, and an opportunity to vegetate and to rest his weary mind and body was his at last. On the 1st of June he had informed his wife that unless he had time to think he could not possibly hope to win the award in the coming competition for the Public Library building at Foxburgh. On this Mrs. Nichols had set her heart. To tell the truth, they were both tired—tired of the bustle and rush of city life, from the rumble of the milkman's cart over the pavement in the early morning to the clang of the fire-engine as it jangled round the corner at dead of night. They needed rest—rest from calls and newspapers and five-o'clock teas and telephones and stock quotations and servants and marriages and deaths and late suppers and small-talk. And they had found it at last, here on this abandoned farm, a good twenty miles from the meretricious excitement and vitiated atmosphere of town.

It was the Fourth of July, and yet there was scarcely a sound to be heard. The very bees neglected to hum. The children were in the barn, scraping acquaintance with the live-stock and tumbling in the hay. Their voices sounded pleasantly remote. Before leaving town Tom had made a bargain with them. On the understanding that they would forego fire-crackers and other noisy accompaniments of the national holiday, he had presented them with four rabbits. Mrs. Nichols was upstairs tending the new baby, for a baby has to be looked after on a quiet abandoned farm as carefully as elsewhere. But Tom himself was supremely comfortable.

He had swung his hammock between two apple-trees, the boughs of one of which shaded his head from the sun. He could see everything which went on about the house without even turning his head. There was absolutely nothing on his mind, and he was free to let that important mechanism lie fallow. From time to time he opened his eyes to enjoy the charming outlook. The old homestead, the main portion of which had been built prior to the Revolution, stood picturesquely dilapidated and awry on ground a little higher than the rest of the farm. The rose, honeysuckle, and other vines which blithely ran riot over the front seemed all that saved it from collapse. Yet it was comfortable enough inside. Tom was not altogether sure that he would not find the double bed atrociously hard as soon as the glamour of the situation had faded into every-day reality, but there was no denying that the cream was so thick that it required joggling before it would pour, and that the hearth possessed all the capacity for blazing logs which a hungry city imagination associates with the rustic fireside. To be sure it was now the Fourth of July, when wood fires are apt to be superfluous; but it was pleasant to feel that there was one to light if you wished; and there were the big brass andirons and the curious old bellows, at any rate. On one side of the house stood the barn and the outbuildings, tenanted still by a sow with young ones, some clucking poultry, and a solitary twenty-year-old farm horse, which, under the guidance of Uncle Reuben Coffin, had fetched

Tom and his family from the station the day before. On the other side was a small flower bed, where peonies and dahlias and mignonette and scarlet-runners and other country flowers bloomed in sweet profusion. It had once been a large garden, but since the death of Farmer Joseph Coffin ten years before it had gradually dwindled away, and in the field beyond, where oats and barley and cauliflowers and spinach and squashes and strawberries had formerly grown to proud maturity, there were only a patch of corn and a few potato-plants for the immediate needs of the widow Coffin and her daughter and limping Uncle Reub.

But only a countryman's eye would have noted that the farm was out at elbows. To Tom, as he lay in his hammock, the landscape seemed a paradise. The fields rolled away in green freshness, with here and there a stretch of woodland, to a horizon of stately hills, and on every side were peace and stillness. He could just discern the silver line of a stream threading its way through the distance. In front of the house stood a genuine moss-bound, old-fashioned well with buckets, and by the barn was a kennel, in front of which

Pop, the huge mastiff, stiff with age and rheumatism, lay basking, with his head upon his paws. Tom said to himself that he had been longing in his inner consciousness for years for some such refuge as this, and he had now merely to close his eyes and enjoy the situation to his heart's content. A book —a volume of poems—lay on his lap, but Tom had no inclination to read. He would fain bask like Pop, and think in a lazy, listless fashion.

What a blessing it was to be in the country on this day of all others! No fire-crackers, no fish-horns, no torpedoes, no crowd! The pensive lowing of the kine and the clucking of an agitated hen were the sole, infrequent invasions of the summer stillness. It had rained on July 1st, and again on July 2d, and the aspect of the skies had caused his brow to pucker on the morning of the third day; but the sun had asserted his majesty at last simultaneously with the arrival of the express-cart at the door. And here they were.

A sound of a closing door caused Tom to open his eyes again. The disturber was Uncle Reuben Coffin, or Uncle Reub, as everyone called him, who was standing on the door-sill in his Sunday go-to-meeting trousers, shirt, necktie, and suspenders, but without a coat. The old man was lame. One of his legs was shorter than the other. He walked by the aid of a stick, and his gait was a jerky hobble. He cast a furtive glance in Tom's direction, and began to work toward him. Uncle Reub was the man of the house. He was a half-brother of Joseph Coffin, and had lived with the widow and her daughter Maretta ever since his brother's death. Both Reuben and Joseph were veterans of the civil war, and both had come out of it without a scratch. Joseph had succumbed to liver-complaint ten years ago, but Reuben's injury dated back to the year immediately following that in which he had left the service. He had fallen from the hay-loft in the barn and fractured his leg. Last evening he had more than satisfied Tom's curiosity regarding him by a detailed account of the accident, which in Uncle Reuben's estimation furnished ample grounds for a government pension. As he explained to Tom, it grew out of the war. If he had not enlisted he would never have remained on the farm, for his tastes as a lad had been roving, and his eyes had been fixed on the far West when Fort Sumter fell. Oh yes, it grew straight out of the war, and if ever a man was entitled to a pension it was he. He had petitioned Congress in vain until now, but this new bill would settle matters, and he hoped to have his papers signed before the maple-leaves turned.

Although Uncle Reub had satisfied Tom's curiosity, Tom still remained a mystery to him. The old man's furtive glance seemed to express wonder why a young man who had the chance to hear fire-crackers, and see the balloon and the military, should prefer to lie in a hammock with his eyes shut on the Fourth of July. Shyness had restrained his tongue last evening from asking questions of the new boarders, but here was an opportunity not to be neglected. First he hobbled over to the open barn, in order to avoid the appearance of premeditation, and busied himself for a few moments in examining once more the two bicycles belonging to Tom and his wife which stood just inside. Then he made for Tom.

Tom, who was fully aware of his presence,

was tempted to simulate slumber. He had no wish for conversation; indeed, he yearned for solitude. But city people have the habit of politeness even toward those whom they wish to avoid, and custom was too much for him. He sat up and nodded at Uncle Reub, who stood leaning against the apple-tree toward which Tom was stretched.

"Suffering from lung trouble, ain't yer?" said the old man, tentatively.

"Not to my knowledge."

"Sweat much nights?"

"I haven't begun to yet."

Uncle Reuben felt of his chin, and pondered. "I had a cousin jus' your build who died o' consumption two years back come the fifteenth day of next month. He sweat nights dreadful. The doctors said it warn't no use trying to do for him. Yer cough some, don't yer?"

"Not at all. I never had a cough in my life, Mr. Coffin, and my lungs were examined for life-insurance six months ago, and pronounced perfectly sound."

"I want to know!" said the old man, who felt in no wise rebuffed by this downright refutation of his theory. He was merely do-

ing his best to express friendly interest, and to become better acquainted. "Old Billy has gone dead lame this morning," he continued, by way of a second attempt. Old Billy was the aged farm horse of the family already referred to.

"I'm afraid that bringing us from the station was too much for him," said Tom. "I'm sorry to hear it."

"I expect it's rheumatism. He's liable to spells of it. But it's kind of provoking for me and Maretta. We'd fixed to drive over Foxburgh way to see the celebration. I reckon now a bi-cy-cle don't go lame?" he added, with a facetious glance at the two machines.

If there was a theme capable of arousing Tom from his present delicious torpor, Uncle Reuben had hit upon it. Tom was just beginning to ride a bicycle. Not only Tom, but Mrs. Nichols. They were in the throes of acquiring facility, and delighted with their budding talent. A strong argument in favor of retiring to the country had been the expectation of being able to practise in obscurity, and witch the world with this substitute for noble horsemanship on their return to town. Tom had waked up one morning and announced that he was going to buy a bicycle, and a fortnight later Mrs. Nichols had taken the bit between her teeth and declared that she would ride too. It had been a little difficult for Tom to get rid of the conviction which he had acquired by personal observation that pretty women do not ride wheels, but his better half's reply that he would soon behold one was extremely pertinent. "It is all a matter of clothes, dear," she had explained to Tom. "Wait until you see me, and I'm sure you'll be satisfied. Besides, only think how delightful it will be to have me with you on your rides, instead of poking off all by yourself." The event had justified her statement. They both were still at the wobbly stage; but there was no doubt in Tom's mind that Mrs. Nichols on a bicycle was fully as charming as Mrs. Nichols on foot. And when a husband is satisfied, cannot a woman afford to smile in the face of a critically conservative world?

Consequently Tom raised himself a little in the hammock in order to obtain a more complete proud glimpse at the precious machines, and his expression brightened as he answered :

"A bicycle is the poor man's friend, Mr. Coffin. It isn't afraid of railroad trains or electric cars; and if it goes lame it doesn't eat its head off while recovering."

Mr. Coffin sighed. It might be that he was deploring his game-leg, which stood in the way of his ever mounting a wheel, or it might be that he was reflecting on the wide difference just pointed out by Tom between a lame horse and a lame bicycle in the matter of feeding. He again felt of his chin meditatively.

"How much might one of them machines cost, if it ain't asking too much?" he inquired.

"One hundred and fifty dollars for the best. But you can get a good second-hand one for seventy-five."

"Most as much as for a fair to middlin' horse."

"But there's no expense for oats, or distemper, or breakage, no veterinary bills, and no cost for shoeing and sharpening. Besides, bicycles must come down in price, Mr. Coffin. It's merely a question of time. The American people intend to ride."

Tom's enthusiasm so far got the better of

him that he grasped the sides of the hammock and sat up and looked at his tormentor; then suddenly remembering why he was there, he sank back emphatically, and closed his eyes again.

A countryman is slow to take a hint. Besides, Tom's momentary flow of words had been reassuring. Uncle Reuben waited a moment, then he said:

"They're cute things, sure. Speakin' now of inventions, what might be yer opinion about these 'ere rain-makers?"

Not a sound came from the hammock. Uncle Reuben waited for a reasonable time, but he did not seem to be disturbed by his failure to obtain an answer. He varied his posture a little and glanced up at the sky, shielding his eyes with his hand.

"It's great weather for the Fourth of July," he remarked.

This was the sort of observation which did not strictly require an answer. It might pass for a soliloquy. A man might make it and not get a response without loss of self-respect. Not even a murmur came from the hammock. Uncle Reuben cocked an eye again skyward, hitched his suspenders into place, and saying, by way of explanation, " I guess I'll go and fix up the scarecrow," halted off in the direction of the corn-patch.

As may have been manifested by his burst of declaration regarding the American people, Tom was at heart a patriot and a believer in the institutions of his native country. Ordinarily the conventional celebration of the Fourth of July had no more terrors for him than for the average adult of forty in his walk of life. He would not have deemed it proper to debar his children from fire-crackers, even by a bribe, if he had not felt that rest was imperative for him in order to win the Foxburgh award. Consequently, although Uncle Reuben was gone, his consciousness, or rather half-consciousness, remained under the spell of their conversation. The weather for the national holiday was indeed glorious, and though he had reason to rejoice that he was removed from the blaze and noise, was it not an inspiring thought that in every city and town of the national domain from the Atlantic to the Pacific an orator was rehearsing in fervid speech the national glories and the national hopes, bands of music were playing, balloons were ascending, and the great

American people was letting itself go? And only think how many bicycles were being ridden within the same ocean-bounded territory! Surely the price of bicycles must come down. Under the influence of these appropriate sentiments Tom fell asleep, and the farm was stiller than ever. Pop slumbered in his kennel, and Uncle Reuben down in the corn-patch sat rigging the scarecrow, keeping his back to the new boarder by way, perhaps, of mild resentment.

The next thing Tom was conscious of was a sound as of cows cropping grass very close to his ear. He struggled against the impression until it changed to a ripping sound, and at the same moment his nose was violently tickled by something hard, a package smote him rudely on the chest, and a voice above him called, "Why in thunder don't you catch hold, you infernal idiot?"

To be called an idiot, especially on the Fourth of July, is galling to a free-born American citizen. Tom's eyes opened simultaneously with the upward spring he made. But he was fairly electrified by what he saw. In front of his face dangled a long rope, and overhead, in close proximity to the apple-tree, was a huge oscillating mass. What could it be? What did it mean? Merciful heavens, it was a balloon—a real, active balloon!

Even a patriot can be rendered incapable of action by astonishment and the complexity of his emotions. Where had it come from? Was it coming down on him? What had the bale of cannon crackers, which had nearly broken his breast-bone, to do with it? What did the two men in the swaying car, ten feet above the apple-tree, wish him to do? There was quite a breeze now, and they were bellowing like mad.

"Catch hold of the rope, can't you?"

Tom glared at the speaker, nevertheless he grabbed at the rope. He was out of the hammock now. He missed it, for it was bobbing just above his head, and the air around him seemed to be raining packages of cannon crackers, rockets, and other missiles of the fireworks order. Apparently the two occupants of the balloon were acting at counter purpose, for one was throwing out everything he could lay his hands on to make the monster rise, whereas the other, who was peering over the edge of the car, was anxious that Tom should grasp the rope so as to

make her fast to the tree. Tom said to himself that it must be the balloon from Foxburgh
which had been sent up that morning, and in
obedience to orders he made another lunge
at the rope. This time he caught it, and he
felt as if he had seized a comet by the tail,
for just at that moment a puff of wind struck
the " George Washington " — he could see
the large letters of her name—and she rolled
and swayed like a ship in a heavy sea, then
swooping away from dangerous proximity to
the apple-tree, began to career in a level line
across the farm. Both the occupants now
were yelling like crazy creatures, but their
words were inaudible to Tom. For an instant
he ran like a deer-hound, holding fiercely to
the rope ; the next he was lifted from his
feet, and hung dangling, with his toes a few
inches from the ground. A huge portmanteau just missed him and burst open at his
feet, and two bags of sand fell with dull thuds
on either side.

In an instant the abandoned farm awoke
to action. The mastiff Pop bounded along at
Tom's heels, barking wildly. Tom's four
children, lured from the hay by the hubbub,
stood open-mouthed, paralyzed at the sight

of their father being dragged along by this
monster of the air. It was not until Mrs.
Nichols, with the baby in her arms, flew from
the house, crying "Tom! Tom! Tom!" that
they added their shrill voices to the tumult,
and scurried over the pasture in pursuit. In
their wake hobbled, as fast as he was able,
Uncle Reuben, giving vent to his emotion in
a frantic "Whoa, there!—whoa, there!—
whoa, there!" And last, but not least, the
widow Coffin and Maretta flitted along behind,
screaming like two agitated geese, their necks
extended, and their white aprons fluttering
in the breeze.

Tom does not know to the present day exactly why he held on like grim death; but he
did, though the huge balloon rolled and
pitched and surged, so that occasionally he
was lifted three feet from the ground, and it
looked as if he would be carried up a mile or
two with even greater promptitude than
Sindbad the Sailor was borne away by the
predatory roc in the "Arabian Nights'" tale.
And all the time it was raining, not cats and
dogs, but what were much more unwelcome
to Tom—bunches of fire-crackers in mad
profusion, as though fate was determined to

foist the Fourth of July upon him in spite of everything. He could not see very distinctly, for he was spinning round like a teetotum, so that he got only what might be called bird's-eye glimpses. He did discern quite clearly for an instant his better half in the van of his pursuers, waving the baby in her arms in wild dismay, and he made one last frantic effort to pull down the balloon before letting go. Just then there was another ripping sound, which resembled the bursting of an enormous torpedo, and Tom felt his feet touch earth again. In the next instant he narrowly dodged a collision with an elm-tree, and immediately after his course was rudely stayed, and he found himself being wound round and round the venerable trunk. When he came to a halt the balloon and the top of the elm-tree seemed to have amalgamated, and the voice which had but lately dubbed him an infernal idiot now shouted from a stalwart bough, "You're a noble fellow, sir — a genuine hero, worthy of the day we celebrate."

Thereupon the speaker, with an agile movement, swung himself from his perch and dropping close to Tom, threw his arms about his neck.

"Your hand, sir, your hand."

Tom, who still was grasping the end of the rope, which was wound around the tree, being of a forgiving disposition, let go, and suffered his fingers to be grasped by the enthusiastic stranger.

"You're a hero, sir. The country shall know of this. Permit me to introduce myself."

The young man—he was a thin, nervous-looking, snappy-eyed individual of about thirty, with a prominent Roman nose—fumbled in his vest-pocket and produced a printed card. Tom read the inscription with a feeling akin to horror: "Irving K. Baker, Foxburgh *Mail and Gazette.*"

"The most enterprising newspaper in the United States. Have you a cabinet photograph of yourself, sir, on the premises?"

The necessity of answering this question was averted for the moment by the arrival, in a breathless condition, of Mrs. Nichols, who threw herself and the baby upon Tom in one warm indiscriminate embrace.

Mr. Baker's hat was off in an instant, and he jumped and changed feet. "Your lady, sir?"

"This is my wife, Mrs. Thomas Nichols. Elizabeth, this is Mr.—er—Irving K. Baker, one of the gentlemen in the balloon."

"Charmed to make your acquaintance, Mrs. Nichols. Allow me, madam, to congratulate you on the noble act of heroism just performed by your husband. At great personal risk he has guided the course of the ill-fated 'George Washington,' which rose an hour ago in Foxburgh amid the shouts of thousands of free-born American citizens, so successfully that Professor Strout and myself have been enabled to seek refuge in the branches of this noble elm at a moment when instant destruction seemed to stare us both in the face."

"Where is Professor Strout?" inquired Elizabeth, who was of a practical turn of mind nothwithstanding her extreme devotion to her husband. As for Tom, his attention had been momentarily diverted by the sight of his children, all of whom, after realizing that the race was over, had stopped to gather up the fireworks which Mr. Irving Baker had let fall, and were now moving swiftly toward him with laden pockets and arms.

"I am safe, madam, and will be down in a

moment," said the professor, answering for himself from the summit of the tree. Tom and his wife, gazing eagerly through the foliage, beheld a pleasant-looking man, of about the same age as Mr. Baker, absorbed in grappling with the remains of the collapsed air-monster.

"One of the most celebrated aeronauts in the country," explained the reporter. "This is his twenty-sixth voyage, and he has never broken a limb."

"What was the matter with the balloon?" inquired Mrs. Nichols.

"She burst, madam, in mid-air, not once, but twice, and, had our course not been providentially guided by your husband, the probabilities are that we should now be lying inanimate within a short distance from this spot. Where are we, by-the-way?"

"You're on the widow Coffin's farm," said Uncle Reuben, who, in company with the two females of his family, had just hobbled up in time to answer this inquiry.

"I expect we'll be able to take our Fourth of July dinner with you," continued Mr. Baker, suavely, addressing Mrs. Coffin, with a quick perception that she was the mistress of the situation. He glanced at the same time so admiringly at Maretta that the country lass looked up and then down.

"How many be you?" asked the widow.

"Two. Professor Strout and myself."

"There's a goose and apple sass and a plum pudding. I guess you're welcome," replied Mrs. Coffin.

"Can we have these, sir?" broke in Tom's eldest boy of eleven, indicating the spoils which he and his brothers had collected.

"Bless your hearts, yes. We'll let the crackers off after dinner, and in the evening we'll have a genuine Fourth of July fireworks show, with rockets and booms and Catherine-wheels."

"Bully for you!" cried the children together, and Maretta let slip a gratified "Oh, my!"

"We haven't had any fire-crackers to-day," said the eldest boy.

"What's that?" cried Mr. Baker, with an astonished and suspicious glance at Tom. "Are you an Englishman?"

"No, sir. It was an accident. They usually have plenty."

"My advent, then, is a peculiarly fortunate circumstance," answered Irving K. Baker.

A few minutes later the entire party was on its way to the farm-house in the gayest of spirits. That is, all except Tom. He lagged a little behind, reflecting that his day was completely spoiled, and that even on an abandoned farm a man is not safe from the Fourth of July. They were clearly in for a noisy time ; and nobody, not even his wife, was disposed to sympathize with him on the subject. What with the heroism of her husband, and the escape of the occupants of the balloon, and the happiness of her children, and the blithe spirits of Mr. Irving K. Baker, and last, but not least, the pathetic tenor voice of Professor Alvin Strout, who had come down from the tree-top with the remains of the late " George Washington," trolling plaintively a stanza of " Oh, why should the spirit of mortal be proud ? " Mrs. Nichols was in a state of pleased excitement. As for Maretta, it was obvious that she was at loss to decide whether the professor was " a more elegant gentleman " than the reporter, or *vice versa*. The professor was inclined to be stout, and he had a wavy dark-

brown mustache and curly hair, which gave
him a more fetching appearance than Mr.
Baker, who was lean and smooth-shaven.
Maretta, who walked in front with the reporter, kept casting sheep's eyes over her
shoulder at the professor, by way of holding
them both in tow. The professor walked
with Mrs. Nichols, to whom he related his
entire personal history before they reached
the farm-house. It appeared that he came
of a family of balloonists. His father and
grandfather had each been noted aeronauts,
and the latter had been drowned in the Bay
of Biscay after an explosion very similar to
that which had worked the ruin of the late
"George Washington." The professor, not
unnaturally, was a little lachrymose over the
loss of his balloon, in which he had made four
successful trips already. She had burst the
first time without warning just over the spot
where Mr. Nichols had been slumbering;
but, though Mr. Baker had been eager to de-
scend at this juncture, the professor himself
had done his best to continue his voyage
until the second catastrophe had proved the
futility of his endeavor.

"But I have nothing to reproach myself

with," he concluded, wiping his eyes. " Although I am accustomed to fall on my feet, it appears that I have been more than usually fortunate on this occasion," he added, with a gallant bow.

Mrs. Nichols had it on the tip of her tongue to remark that he would be sure to fall on his head some day instead of his feet, but she reflected that, as he was a balloonist by profession, there was really no use in pointing out its dangers at a time when he was already depressed. They had now reached the house, where the atmosphere was rife with the savor of roast goose, which so far restored the spirits of the professor that he rubbed his hands cheerily together, and presently began to perform some acts of legerdemain, ostensibly for the amusement of the children, but it may be with an eye to Maretta also. He seized two of the new rabbits, and with a deft movement of his fingers rolled them into one, proceeded to swallow the compound animal, and then shook them both from Mr. Irving Baker's hat. The children shrieked with pleasure, and Maretta said, " Oh, my! ain't he cute ? " so many times that Mr. Baker felt called upon to play a solo on a jews-harp and dance a jig to avoid sinking into obscurity.

"Tom," whispered Mrs. Nichols, observing that her husband had retired to a corner, where he was sitting in glum despair, "here is an occasion for the display of moral courage to serve as a pendant to your physical bravery of the morning. Cheer up. He really plays uncommonly well, and the professor actually made my heart leap into my mouth when he rolled the two bunnies into one."

"That Baker will have us all in his confounded newspaper to-morrow morning. I see it in his eye. To think, Elizabeth, of what our Fourth of July was intended to be, and then consider what it is! I almost wish I had let the 'George Washington'——"

"Dinner!" exclaimed the widow Coffin, entering from the kitchen, and cutting short thereby Tom's dire malediction.

"Be brave," whispered his wife. "It cannot last long, and if the goose only holds out we shall do famously."

A phrase of tender conjugal appeal is often more effective than a page of Scripture.

Tom clinched his teeth and seized the

" I ALMOST WISH I HAD LET THE GEORGE WASHINGTON—"

carving-knife. "I will do my best, dear," he murmured.

Tom's best was very good indeed. He carved the goose with consummate skill, so that everyone had enough, and at the first mention of the word Fourth of July he rose from the table, and reappeared with sundry bottles of ale from his private stock, in which a variety of toasts appropriate to the occasion, proposed in a very witty fashion by Mr. Baker, were drunk. Then the professor sat down at the piano and sang "The Lost Chord," and Mr. Baker, to cap the climax, recited Poe's "Raven," without the slightest provocation excepting the ale in question. Maretta, who waited at table, and who had been in a state of concentrated giggle over the humorous portion of the programme, was now in tears, and Uncle Reuben confided to Tom that "them two were better'n the theātre, and, barrin' the absence of wild animals, most as good as a circus." The professor, to prove, perhaps, that he had his lighter side in song as well as real life, then supplemented "The Lost Chord" with a negro ditty, which captivated everybody, especially Mrs. Coffin.

"He's just real comical," she said, in a stage-whisper. "It's too bad," she added to the company, with a pathetic air, "Maretta ain't got no accomplishments."

All eyes were directed toward the young woman in question, who flushed becomingly, and who, as so many young women in her position with accomplishments would have done, said nothing tart to her mother in reply. She merely looked down, much to the disgust both of the professor and Mr. Baker, whose glances plainly declared that they were prepared to think none the less of her on that account. She was really a very pretty girl, save for the bang which disfigured her comeliness, and she had taken advantage of a few moments which had intervened between the reporter's performance on the jews-harp and dinner to put on a pale blue silk frock.

"For my part, Mrs. Coffin, I think that she is to be heartily congratulated because she hasn't any," said Tom, by way of commentary on the widow's grievance.

This was the only speech of doubtful propriety of which Tom was guilty, and its effect was speedily counteracted by the cigars

"DINNER!"

which he presented at this juncture to the two performers, who had cast suspicious looks in his direction.

"You are a gentleman and a scholar, sir," said Mr. Baker, with affable satisfaction as he accepted the proffered Regalia Britannica. "If your young Americans would like to fire off those cannon crackers I am entirely at their and your service."

For the next fifteen minutes the abandoned farm was one of the noisiest spots in the universe. When the last pop had been uttered and the smoke was clearing away, Mr. Irving Baker announced that he would devote his energies to erecting a frame-work for the rockets and Catherine-wheels to be discharged after dark, and he said to Professor Strout,

"I will match you, Alvin, to see whether you or I go to the wood-pile for an axe and lumber."

Thereupon the reporter drew from his pocket his mascot, an old-fashioned United States cent, which he flipped into the air.

"If you are to match me, mine's a head," said the professor, who had a Mexican dollar as the genius of his fortunes.

10

"I have done it," said Mr. Baker, triumphantly, and he glanced contentedly in the direction of Maretta. There was a corresponding look of depression on the countenance of the baffled magician as, accompanied by the children and Uncle Reuben, he proceeded toward the barn. Who knows but he was reflecting that a stroke of legerdemain would, under the circumstances, have been wiser than trusting to that bawd, Fortune?

Seeing Mr. Baker and Maretta compose themselves on the door-step, Mrs. Nichols whispered in Tom's ear: "You have been a hero twice to-day, dear boy. Go upstairs and try to get forty winks. I am certain that every fire-cracker has been set off, and I will take baby to the barn."

Tom did as he was bid. The consciousness of virtue is apt to be its own reward. He fell asleep almost instantly, and his slumber was pleasantly agitated by a promising idea for the library at Foxburgh. He had slept just ten minutes when this vision was rudely interrupted by a hand laid on his shoulder.

"Why in thunder——" he began.

"Tom, dear, I'm awfully sorry, but I had

"MINE'S A HEAD," SAID THE PROFESSOR

to wake you. Professor Strout has fallen from the loft in the barn and broken his leg."

Tom sat up and rubbed his eyes. Even the serious nature of this announcement did not restrain him from exclaiming, "I was just getting a grand idea for the library, and now I've lost it. Confound the professor and the Fourth of July! What did you say Elizabeth? Broken his leg? Poor fellow! How did he manage to do that?"

"He was looking for a suitable piece of wood for the rocket-stand, and he fell over backward at almost the same point as Uncle Reuben Coffin fell years ago."

"Now that's a queer coincidence, isn't it?" said Tom.

"Yes. They need you to help move him to the house."

"To think," said Tom, as he slipped on his coat, "that a man should drop with a balloon and get off scot-free, and within two hours break his leg by falling from an everyday commonplace barn loft!"

"Isn't it odd!" But Mrs. Nichols was more interested in the live features of the case. "What are we to do, Tom?" she added earnestly. "The nearest doctor is at Middleborough, which is ten miles from here. The horse is lame, you know."

"So he is." Tom stopped on his way downstairs. "If he has really broken his leg, I shall go for the doctor on my wheel."

"Oh, Tom, you haven't had experience enough. You would never get there."

"I shall go. We can't let him die on our hands." There was a sort of fierce fervor in his tone.

"This is a fine outfit," exclaimed Mr. Baker, who met them at the barn door. "A sad ending to a delightful day."

Tom passed in and found a dismal little group bending over the prostrate form of the unfortunate balloonist, who was lying on an improvised hay bed.

"Papa, papa," cried the children, "the gentleman who swallowed the rabbits has hurt himself."

"His leg's broke and the bone's protrudin'. He struck the floor three inches to the south'ard of where I fell twenty years back," explained Uncle Reuben.

"I guess it's nothing to worry over," said the victim, but the effort of turning slightly to look at Tom distressed him so greatly that he groaned. "Can't walk to the house, though."

"No; we're going to carry you," said his friend. "You'll feel better as soon as we get you on a soft bed." He murmured to Tom, "It's a pretty poor lookout with the doctor ten miles off and the farm-horse lame."

"Yes," replied Tom. "Do you ride a bicycle?"

"Nop."

Tom said nothing further at the moment, but, after they had deposited the professor on Mrs. Coffin's bed, he leaned over him and said: "I'll have the doctor here in a jiffy. I'm going for him on my wheel."

"Oh, my!" said Maretta.

"Tom," said Mrs. Nichols, following him to the door, "if you're going, I'm going too."

"Nonsense, dear."

"It's ten miles. Supposing anything should happen to you? You've never ridden more than half a mile before at a time."

"Neither have you."

"No; but if anything should happen, we should be together. Oh, Tom, I must go. Besides, it will be moonlight coming home."

"Or broad daylight."

Mr. Baker, who had followed them down the staircase listening to the conversation, took out his note-book with a graphic air. "It seems to me a most charming idea that your wife should accompany you. It will add a peculiarly picturesque feature to the extraordinary incidents of the day, which I intend to describe at full length in a special article in the columns of the Foxburgh *Mail and Gazette*."

"How dare you, sir?" exclaimed Tom, turning upon him with the sudden ire of one who has been goaded beyond his strength, and grasping him by the sleeve. "How dare you threaten to describe the personal affairs of myself and Mrs. Nichols in the public press? I have put up with enough to-day already, but this is the last straw. Promise me that you will not allude to me or mine in any manner whatsoever, or I will not stir one step on this errand."

"Tom, Tom," whispered Mrs. Nichols, "you forget yourself. Do not spoil all after you have acted so splendidly."

Mr. Baker had torn himself loose from Tom's grasp, and stood with folded arms, the picture of haughty contempt, waiting for this outburst to terminate. Then he said :

"You are an enemy of the institutions of your country, sir. My suspicions were already aroused, but I am sure of it now. You are out of sympathy with the fitting celebration of this glorious day ; you have hidden in the country, and refused fire-crackers to your children ; you sneer at popular diversions ; and last, and worst, you would muzzle the liberty of the press. You are an aristocrat, sir, a cold-blooded aristocrat. But the great democratic press snaps its fingers at you."

"Mr. Baker," protested Mrs. Nichols, with engaging mien, "my husband is tired and run down ; he has come to this place for his health, and the many exciting events of the day have worn upon him. He did not mean what he said, believe me. We are going for the doctor of course, and we feel nothing but the kindest sentiments toward you and Professor Strout ; but—but can't you understand that to people who have no taste for publicity the idea of being described in the newspapers as bicycle - riders on an errand of mercy would be very annoying, especially if it were illustrated ? "

"Of course it would be illustrated," said Baker, "and in our best style. I believed you would like it, madam." There was disappointment in his tone.

The interruption by his wife had given Tom time to think. "I beg your pardon," he said, extending his hand. "I had no right to speak as I did. As Mrs. Nichols has said to you, my nerves are unstrung. Pray accept my apologies, and after the doctor has been brought here we will discuss this further."

Mr. Baker's eyes lighted up with the gleam of generosity. "I am happy to withdraw the epithets which I used in the heat of controversy," he said, as he returned the handshake.

"Odious miscreant and interloper!" muttered Tom five minutes later as he mounted his machine.

"'Sh!" answered Elizabeth. "Don't, for Heaven's sake, agitate me now, dear, for if I should fall before these people it would be the crowning stroke, and I do feel wobbly."

The two riders worked their way along the highway with careful deliberation, followed by the plaudits not only of their children,

"MY HUSBAND IS TIRED AND RUN DOWN"

but of the rest of the company. They could hear Uncle Reuben limping after them in his unwillingness to lose sight of them, and telling them the route for the fifth time.

"We can't expect not to come to grief before long," continued Elizabeth, "but I do hope that nothing will happen until we get round the bend. Don't go quite so fast, Tom, dear."

"I suppose," said Tom, with a sigh, "that I was a fool to get mad. He and I look at things from entirely different points of view. I loathe the Fourth of July and he loves it, and he says I'm a cold-blooded aristocrat. I'm willing to die for my country, but why should my wife and children be paraded in the newspapers?"

"And on bicycles, too! Oh, Tom, can you blow your nose?"

"No."

"Neither can I. I wonder if I shall ever be able to ride with one hand? And some people use neither. I think they're both taken by Maretta—don't you?"

"She's too good for them."

"Not a bit. You're prejudiced, Tom. I think they're rather nice. Mr. Baker's just the sort of man who is liable to become President of the United States, and a girl might well think twice before refusing an aeronaut who could be a necromancer when business was dull. Oh, Tom, are you going to coast?"

Tom was. "We shall never get there if we don't. It looks like a smooth hill."

Up went their feet, and down they went. Elizabeth gave a little shriek, which was partly joy and partly apprehension, when they were half-way down.

On they went with increasing confidence. A fly flew straight into Elizabeth's eye, and in pain and bewilderment she clapped one hand to the spot, and in another instant came rudely in contact with a fence at the road-side. But this might happen to anyone, she remarked, after she had remounted. It was an exquisite afternoon. The sunset clouds were beginning to variegate the west, and the landscape was a delight to behold. The loosening of one of the nuts in Tom's machine caused a delay of fifteen minutes. Presently it became necessary to pump air into one of the pneumatic tires. But these were trifles, and on they went.

"Why do you keep chirruping to your wheel as if it were a horse?" asked Elizabeth presently.

"Because I can't forget that it isn't a horse. When that train went by a few minutes ago I expected it to rear. When I wish it to go faster I say 'click,' and feel like an idiot a moment after."

They stopped at a farm-house for some milk, and learned that they had covered one-half of the distance in a little less than an hour, including stops. Ten minutes later the sun went down.

"Now it will be cooler and more poetic," said Elizabeth. "Do I look like a guy, Tom?"

"No; you are perfectly sweet."

"That was lovely of you, even if it was a white lie. When the moon comes out it will be heavenly."

"Look," cried Tom, pointing to the horizon, where the streak of the first rocket indicated that the American people were still hard at work. Ten minutes later the whole sky was alive with distant fireworks variegated by heat-lightning. Ten minutes later Elizabeth's machine broke down. It happened without warning, and the break was radical and comprehensive. Their combined mechanical resources were put utterly to confusion. What were they to do? They sat upon a fence to ponder the matter.

"You must go on," said Elizabeth, firmly.

"And leave you behind?"

"That poor man must have a doctor."

"You might go and let me stay."

"No; a woman riding a bicycle alone at dead of night would be worse than a woman sitting on a fence. I will stay here."

"But, Elizabeth, supposing something or some one should——"

"Pooh!" she interrupted. "As for some-things, there are no bears or lions; and as for some ones, all the tramps must have gone to town to see the fireworks. When the moon gets up it will not even be pokey. I shall sit on this fence and poetize until you return. Kiss me, dear, and go."

Tom obeyed. His embrace suggested a little that he might be parting with her forever, but he had no arguments wherewith to refute her logic. Once under way his apprehensions lent velocity to his pace. He took chances, and therefore two headers. But he made slightly better time. He was sore, dirty, and tired when he reached the doctor's house, which looked forbiddingly dark. It was half past eight. The doctor must have gone to bed, or more probably to see the fireworks in the town, which were in full blaze when Tom arrived. He dismounted and rang. Presently the window was thrown open, and a head appeared.

"Holloa, there!"

"Is Dr. Hopkins at home?"

"I'm the doctor. What'll you have?" said a cheery voice.

Tom explained his needs.

"The widow Coffin's farm? That's the end of everything, isn't it? And I was just trying to forget that I had attended seven cases of singed young America and two cases of 'didn't know it was loaded' since the sun rose on this glorious anniversary. I'll be down in a minute."

It was barely five minutes before the doctor opened the door. He was tall and athletic looking. "My wife, my children, my hired man, and my hired girl have all gone to see the fireworks," he said, "so you'll excuse my not letting you in sooner. I saw you were on

a bicycle, so I'm in bicycle rig too. It's a
fine night for a spin. I think nothing of
twenty miles."

"Yes," said Tom, with a gasp. "Excuse
me—er—there's a lady in the case."

"I thought you said it was a man."

"A man has broken his leg, but my wife is
sitting on a fence half-way between here and
the farm."

"Anything serious?" said Dr. Hopkins,
who from this description jumped at the conclusion that there must be two patients instead of one.

"I mean that my wife's bicycle has broken
down, and I had to come on alone, and—and
if we ride back on bicycles, what is to become
of her?"

"Oh, I see. That's easily solved. I'll
hitch up the bay and drive instead, and pick
up your wife on the way. Or, no," added
the doctor, slapping his thigh, "there's a
better way still; I'll take your bicycle, and
tell the lady that you're coming." Thereupon he began to strap his bag of implements
on to Tom's machine.

"I'm very grateful, I'm sure," said Tom,
who had been wondering how he should be

able to keep pace with the doctor on a wheel.
The doctor might think nothing of twenty
miles, but ten had taken all the wind and energy out of him. A half-hour later he caught
sight at last of a solitary figure perched on a
fence, and realized that Elizabeth was where
he had left her.

"Well, dear," she cried, as he drew in the
quiet, plodding nag, "here I am safe and
sound. You don't know how my heart
throbbed with envy as I beheld the doctor
flying toward me. I thought it was you, and
I said to myself, 'How splendidly he rides!'
And I never realized it wasn't you until he
rode up to me and said, 'This must be Mrs
Nichols.' Do you suppose we shall ever be
able to ride as he does?"

"And nothing harmed you?" asked Tom,
avoiding the question.

"Nothing worse than a bat. And I thought
I smelled a—polecat. It was lovely though,
Tom; so peaceful and poetic. The fence was
a little hard, but I was afraid to lie down for
fear of creeping things. What time is it,
dear?" she asked, as she settled back in the
comfortable vehicle, while Tom carefully concealed the broken bicycle behind the fence.

"A little after nine."

Elizabeth was silent for a few moments; then she said, "An ordinary horse and buggy are really very satisfactory in the long-run, after all."

"I should think they were," said Tom, as he took the reins.

They were not long in reaching the abandoned farm which they now called home. Mr. Baker met them at the gate on arrival. He was in high spirits, for Dr. Hopkins had agreed to carry him as far as their ways were the same, and he would be in Foxburgh in time to print the article which he had written for the morning paper. He said that the professor was as comfortable as could be expected, and that the fracture was nothing out of the common run of broken legs, but that prompt medical attendance had doubtless saved him from pain and the risk of serious complications.

"I beg to offer you, both on his behalf and on mine, the heartiest thanks for your philanthropic and generous assistance," continued Mr. Baker, with fervor, as they walked toward the house after the horse had been hitched. "But for your night ride of mercy my friend's

A SOLITARY FIGURE PERCHED ON A FENCE

leg might have been lost to him forever, if not his life endangered. While the free press of this country yields neither to threats nor to pressure, a noble action is never lost upon it. Permit me to inform you that there is not the slightest allusion to either of you in the chronicle of the day's adventure which I have prepared during your absence." He produced as he spoke a roll of manuscript, which he held out rhetorically. "The omission will be a loss to literature, and a manifest renunciation of the legitimate fruits of journalistic enterprise, but I take the responsibility upon my own shoulders."

Mr. Baker's tones were those of one who feels that he is making a sacrifice, but yet is willing and glad to make it. His thin, nervous face looked solemn and impressive in the moonlight.

"It's very kind of you, I am sure," said Mrs. Nichols.

"Yes, indeed, we're very much obliged to you," murmured Tom.

They both felt like guilty wretches.

"Don't mention it," said Mr. Baker, with a wave of his hand.

He still remained outside, while Tom and

11

his wife went upstairs to make sure that the children had been properly looked after and to inquire for the invalid. They found the professor in the possession of the Coffin family, who were bent on making him comfortable. His leg had been set, and the doctor was on the eve of departure. The children, who were still awake, were loud in their praises of Mr. Baker's display of fireworks.

"I feel somehow as though that man had sacrificed his principles for us, and put us under obligation for life," said Elizabeth to her husband.

"So do I," said Tom, "and yet there is not the slightest reason why we should feel so."

But he went to his drawer, and taking out half a dozen of his best cigars, slipped downstairs. Mr. Baker was still out-doors, and was looking at the moon meditatively.

"Perhaps these will come in pleasantly during your journey," said Tom.

The reporter took the cigars with a bow, and immediately proceeded to light one. Then he put his arm in Tom's, and said, in a whisper,

"Is Maretta keeping company with any-one?"

This was a little disconcerting, but Tom duly found his tongue. "Not to my knowl-edge; but, you know, I arrived only last night."

"True," said Mr. Baker, with an air of gloom. "I beg to inform you, in the strict-est confidence, that I intend to make her Mrs. Irving K. Baker, and I now invite you and your lady to be present at the ceremony, which I hope will take place in the early fall."

"I accept, with pleasure," said Tom, "provided——"

He had been going to say, provided he were still there, but Mr. Baker finished the sentence for him:

"Provided, of course, that no unforeseen obstacles to the match on the part of the young lady arise in the near future."

How often are experiences which we think unfortunate at the time conducive to our ul-timate welfare! If any one had prophesied to Tom Nichols, the architect, when he chose an abandoned farm as a spot where he might meditate on art to advantage, that ultimately he would owe the award in his favor for the Foxburgh Public Library to the acquaintance made by him on the Fourth of July with a reporter who had fallen with a balloon, he would have considered the prophet mad. And yet this proved to be the case, for Irving K. Baker was chosen a member of the City Council of Foxburgh in the following autumn, and subsequently became a member and leading spirit of the Committee on the New Library. Let it be said to Mr. Baker's credit that at the time he voted in favor of Tom's design he had been crossed in love, and was in a doleful state of mind, which in some mortals might have bred a malignant spirit toward all abandoned farms and their occupants. Obstacles on the part of the young lady had arisen, in spite of the fact that the suitor paid weekly visits to the abandoned farm, and sent sundry and frequent gifts of candy and fruit to take the place of his presence. Sad to relate, the professor ate much of the candy and fruit in the course of his prolonged convalescence, and by the time he was well had persuaded the fair Maretta to link her destiny to his. She became Mrs. Alvin Strout on a beautiful

September day. The professor had suggested the appropriateness of being married in midair in a balloon, and offered to provide a clergyman willing to risk the voyage; but Maretta decided in favor of a church. Tom and his wife were present, and they rode to the church on bicycles with amazing swiftness. Tom was rested and five pounds heavier, with his design for the library firmly in his mind's eye. And Mr. Baker was there too, magnanimous to the last. In spite of his feelings he wrote a dazzling account of the nuptials, headed " A Society Wedding on an Abandoned Farm," in which the names of Mr. and Mrs. Thomas Nichols did not appear.

RICHARD AND ROBIN

RICHARD AND ROBIN

MY name is Doddridge—George Harper Doddridge—though it is scarcely important for you to know it, seeing that I am to be merely a chronicler. I am addressed familiarly among my friends and acquaintances as Dodd; but some of the married ones, whose children are encouraged to ride horseback on my either leg as a sort of indemnity for the dinners I consume, call me Uncle George—a pseudonyme which has been adopted also by the younger set at the club. I am the oldest bachelor in the house, and yet I am not so very old. Excepting a grizzly patch on either side, my hair is still dark and abundant as a lad's, save for a bald spot on the crown ; and I can see straight as the crow flies, which all married men of fifty are not able to do. I mention these details merely to demonstrate that I am neither lame, halt, nor blind. And yet they call me Uncle

George. I suppose the reason is because I have been catalogued as a confirmed old bachelor, and consequently am regarded as a safe repository for all sorts of confidences and a convenient object of social charity. It is generally understood that I shall never marry. My story? Pardon me, I intend to keep that one to myself. Yet I will tell you that I am pointed out to young girls in their first season as a constant man, and I have detected in the eyes of more than one of them a look of sympathetic pity, suggestive of a desire to ask me all about it, if they only dared.

I am the oldest bachelor in the house, both in point of years and occupancy. My rooms are the pleasantest of their kind. From one of my parlor windows I command a glimpse of the harbor over the chimney-tops, and from the other see hills green with foliage or white with snow, according to the season. I came here twenty years ago to a small low house where there was accommodation for only four other lodgers. Eight years back this was pulled down, and on the ground formerly covered by it and two adjoining buildings the present towering apartment house was erected. I went around the world

while the work was being done, and on my
return installed myself in my present quarters, where I intend to die. The homelike
feeling which I knew beneath the roof with a
landlady has departed, but I have all the
modern conveniences under the sway of a
janitor; notably plumbing and electricity.
There is a fire-escape at my bed-chamber
window; but if the house burns, I shall burn
with it rather than risk the descent. It is
well enough for the family man to go down
a stepladder in his night-gown at dead of
night; but I have only a nephew, who will
not be inconsolable, to mourn me.

This vicinity is a favorite one for bachelors, and deservedly so, for it is central, and
many things which single men who have to
shift for themselves require are close at hand;
though, come to think of it, the bachelors
were here before the creature comforts, and
the neighborhood has grown up to cater to
our necessities. The three houses which
stood where our apartment-house, the Rexford, now stands were all occupied by single
men, and there were other warrens across the
way and on the same street, out of which or
into which at almost any hour of the day or

night single men were liable to pop. Now
the Rexford shelters all ; and shelters not
merely bachelors, for in the flat immediately
under mine a girl artist lives a blameless life,
and across the entry from hers is the home
of a woman who writes for the society newspapers, and has literary aspirations. Our
little world has become more complex now
that the sphere of woman has widened, and
there is a milliner as well as a florist and an
apothecary in close proximity to the Rexford.
Two doctors have their signs directly opposite, and there is another—a bachelor—in the
house. There is a cabman at the corner, and
altogether I am very well off for a single
man.

Twenty years! They tell me I am growing
set, as all old bachelors do ; and I will admit
that I am more particular than I used to be
about my food, and like to have it at certain
times and piping hot. Still, I can assume as
cheerful a countenance as any man of my age,
or younger, if the dinner hour of my host be
eight o'clock, or some heedless girl fresh from
the nursery makes a mistake of thirty minutes and is a quarter tardy into the bargain.
A man who, like myself, is constantly climb-

ing up and down another's stairs cannot afford
to run amuck too fiercely with the world if
he does not wish to comprehend how much
more bitter in the long-run the club salt is
than any other. Twenty years! In that
time what an army of bachelors I have seen
stepping into life with the down on their
upper lips, and stepping from day to day,
briskly or sadly as the case might be, until
they walked up the aisle with a lover's pride,
or gave up the fight and subsided into middle-aged single men with bald heads! How
many stories I could tell of their doings—
stories sometimes of wedding-cake and for-
get-me-nots, and now of broken hearts and
ruined lives! Here is one:

I used to think blood a delusion, and quite
at odds with democratic doctrine, but the
older I grow the more am I led to believe
that an honorable lineage is the best of heri-
tages. To one who is not a pessimist or a
cynic traditions as to his father's father's
wisdom and his great-grandmother's engaging
charms act as spurs or incentives to noble
effort, even though the lustre of his house
has been dimmed by adversity and its useful-
ness foreshortened by death. I have seen

more than one man in a tight place squeal
like a calf, and have remembered that his
father was a miser, or a coward, or a boor.

Robert Temple came to live in the old
house in the autumn of '71. The somewhat
fantastic nickname Robin, which his mother
gave him when a little boy, had clung to him.
It seemed to suit him. He was a slim, rather
delicate-looking youth, with what was almost
an old-fashioned cast of countenance, and a
figure of the dainty type one associates with
the era of miniatures, flowered waistcoats,
and tight - fitting coats with brass buttons.
His hair was wavy, his expression thoughtful,
and his eyes—dark, eloquent pleaders—were
now wistful, now scintillant with enthusiasm.

I had met him casually before, but with
the indifference a young man is apt to accord
to another several years his junior, and my
real acquaintance dates from the evening
when I, the senior of the house, went up to
pay my respects to the new lodger. His
rooms were over mine, at the top of the house,
and he had been in possession only forty-
eight hours. I can see him now as he looked
when I entered. He was engaged in hanging
up the sword of his father, who fell at Get-

tysburg. As we shook hands the tear which he had brushed off, doubtless, when he heard my knock, moistened my wrist. We talked at first of commonplace things—the merits and demerits of our landlady, and precautions against the too rapid disappearance of coal ; but presently the conversation drifted back to that with which his soul was full.

" You were in the war ? " he asked.

" No ; I enlisted, but typhoid fever laid me low before I was able even to learn the tactics or wear a knapsack."

" I beg your pardon. What a pity ! " he said, softly, as though I had told him of some vital grief which he had molested. " How I envy my father ! " he said, presently. " All puzzling problems were absorbed for him in the opportunity to stand at his post and be shot down for the sake of a great right."

I understood him well. Often had I upbraided Providence for leaving me in the lurch when it gave my contemporaries the chance to satisfy conscience at one fell swoop. And here was another, who had been born too late to claim his part, looking back longingly.

I answered Robin sufficiently in this vein

to show him that I sympathized with him, yet I said, too :

" They are not the only heroes. The world is full of opportunities to-day."

He looked up at me brightly. " I know it," he said. " I ought to be ashamed of myself for repining. I have come here to work hard, Mr. Doddridge."

Glancing around the room, I saw evidences of taste and of an artistic temperament on every side. A variety of prints and etchings, each one of which caught the eye by its merit, were on the walls or ready to hang. Books, knick-knacks, a few pieces of choice pottery, which he had picked up in his two years abroad, were in process of arrangement. Close beside me was a large portfolio.

" Will you let me look at some of your work," I asked, " while you continue your house-furnishing ? "

He seemed pleased, and cleared a space on the table for the portfolio. While I examined his sketches he stood at my elbow, putting in a word of explanation now and again, with a fantastic red and white feather duster over his shoulder. When I had come to the end he began nervously to dust a Japanese tea-tray.

"Temple," I said, presently, delaying a little perhaps to choose my words, loath to praise too much, and yet wishing to express my conviction that he had exceptional talent, "I don't think you need envy anyone. Some of these are delightful. You have a delicacy of fancy of your own which is captivating, and quite unusual. I plume myself on knowing a little something about painting, and so I make bold to give you my opinion."

"It is a limited range, however," he answered, though he flushed with gratification.

"Yes, it is limited, and a little too delicate, perhaps, for popular appreciation; but it is true. And truth is really what we are all striving after, isn't it?"

"Indeed it is. Thank you very much, Mr. Doddridge. You have no idea how encouraging your praise is to me. I was becoming a little downcast. My family does not approve of my art. They let me go abroad, hoping to cure me, and they are disappointed that I have come back with no more taste for business than before."

I remembered that he had two older brothers—John Temple, a coffee merchant, and Samuel Temple, a gentleman farmer, who had married a rich wife.

"Have your brothers seen these sketches?" I inquired.

"Yes. They say they are very pretty. But my brother John seems to think they won't sell. He says I can be a partner in his firm in five years if I only buckle down."

"And are you tempted?"

"If it were not for Dick Benton I should have yielded before this. Don't you know Richard Benton?" he added.

While the question was still on his lips there was a sharp knock at the door, and by an odd coincidence the young man to whom he referred entered. I knew his people, and had seen him as a lad on the streets, as in the case of Robin, but he was practically a new acquaintance. Two men were never more unlike in personal appearance than these two. Richard—or Dick Benton, as the world called him—was a typical square-shouldered, compact, sturdy specimen of humanity, with the bearing already at twenty-five of an alert, shrewd man of affairs. As I learned the next day, he had just started in business for himself downtown. He looked the kind of man who would never tire, has no nerves, and not much imagination, yet of whom one predicates, after the first five minutes, that he has a large fund of horse-sense. There was something refreshingly cheery and wholesome in his demeanor which suggested a steady west wind.

"We scarcely knew each other in college," explained Robin, presently. "We became intimate at one fell swoop, curiously enough, on the Gorner Grat. We went up independently to see the sun rise, and became friends."

"What a morning that was!" said Benton.

"Wasn't it? Not a cloud in the sky, and the mountains gorgeously white with the first snow of the season, which had fallen the afternoon before. Peaks and peaks on every side, and in front of us the Matterhorn towering like a grand, cold goddess. It was sublime."

"You have never done anything better than the sketch you made then while I looked over your shoulder. I expect to be offered ten thousand dollars for that some day, and to refuse it."

"Perhaps," said Robin, with a laugh. "Mr. Doddridge has been looking at my things, Dick, and he has been kind enough to say that they are pretty good."

"Of course they are good," Benton said, as he cut some tobacco for a pipe.

"But Mr. Doddridge is a connoisseur in art."

"And I know nothing about it? Granted. But I know what I like, Robin," he added, defiantly, as he rammed the cavendish in, "and I like your pictures. And I believe if you stick to your paint-brush you will make your reputation."

"And how about starving in the meanwhile?"

"You will not starve," said Benton, quietly.

"I have one thousand dollars a year," he said, addressing me. "On one thousand a year can a man dress like a gentleman, go into society, and keep a yacht or a saddle-horse?"

"Pshaw!" said Benton. "Why should a man who can paint like you think of those things? Leave them to the common clay."

" ' Fame is the spur that the clear spirit doth raise
(That last infirmity of noble minds)
To scorn delights, and live laborious days,' "

I quoted.

Robin looked up at me with a gleam of pleasure. " When you hear me abused, then, as an unpractical visionary fellow who can't earn his salt, you must stand up for me."

I think I understood very well what was working in Robin's mind. He was a sensitive soul, and he wished to have public opinion on his side—that is, the opinion of his general acquaintance, his contemporaries, then chiefly bachelors. He would have winced, for instance, at the patronizing effrontery of David Finn which was addressed to me two or three days later as we walked up the street together. Finn was another of the four lodgers in our house, and a successful stock-broker, though only just thirty, and an exquisite in his appearance and surroundings. He was reputed to have made two hundred thousand dollars by selling stocks which he did not own, or buying stocks which he had not the money to pay for—I forget which; and he carried himself haughtily, as though his father had been a Montague, whereas the story is that he was a sea-captain who retired on the insurance-money which he recovered from a company whose defence was that he had set fire to his own vessel. That was the story, but it may never have been true. Besides, the jury gave him a verdict.

"Holloa, Uncle George, old chappie! What sort is the new inmate? One of those literary fellows, isn't he?"

"He's an artist."

"Oh yes! More money nowadays in painting signs than pictures, isn't there?"

David Finn had a prosperous air, which was rather contagious. Society newspaper scavengers habitually described him as "well-groomed," and he certainly looked as though he had enough to eat and more than enough to drink, and took fully three hundred and sixty-five baths in the course of the year. He was a clever whip, too, and could be seen almost any afternoon on the box of a stylish cart behind a neat-looking cob, as sleek and well groomed as his master. In social matters also he was prominent. He had a way of twisting his mustache which took the place of conversation, and there was no denying his physical comeliness. The mothers of the marriageable girls were wondering whom he would marry.

Robin's die was cast—that is to say, he had definitely decided not to go into the coffee business—and he was hard at work in his studio at the top of our house, which had been adapted to the purpose by cutting a hole in the roof and providing a skylight. I was downtown during the day, but I made a habit of dropping in on him in the evening from time to time to keep track of what he was doing, and every now and then he would turn his canvases which stood against the wall, or draw the covering from his easel to let me see his work. He could not hope, he said, to do enough for an exhibition by the spring, but he expected by the autumn to be ready for the public. Sometimes I met there Richard Benton, who had taken the remaining suite in our house, which had unexpectedly become vacant; frequently, too, David Finn, who was directly opposite Robin, and who when he was at home liked an audience. When Finn was present, as may be surmised, the conversation did not concern art, but

dealt with the operations of syndicates, the
condition of the stock market, speculations
as to how rich A was, and whether B had
made or lost money, the relative speed of
yachts, and the ailments and fine points of
horses. Robin chiefly listened to these re-
citals in a sort of fascinated silence. There
was one topic, however, which they discussed
in common—woman.

I have reference to Robin's state of mind
about Easter-time. It was not until then
that he began to take notice, so to speak, and
to delight to lead the conversation to their
social doings and let it linger there. David
Finn had in his every-day speech a cynical
style where the other sex was concerned.
He knew of at least ten women in society—
not to mention names. "One of the men in
question told me himself, and boasted about
it," he would add, to clinch the credibility of
the matter. But though his attitude in the
abstract was one of suspicion, he was not
without his enthusiasms regarding the young
women of his acquaintance, and though criti-
cal, he could be eloquent concerning individual cases of eyes, and hair, and shoulders.
He and Robin—and, for the matter of that,

Richard—were in the same general social set, and went to much the same entertainments, and many a night David would stroll into Robin's room at one o'clock in the morning after a ball, with a cigar, to talk it over. Occasionally I would make number three. David was prone to descant upon the fine points of the girls he admired in much the same way as he described with enthusiasm the fine points of a horse. Robin would listen to him, and aid and abet him, never hinting at the lateness of the hour, in the hope that sooner or later the name of Gertrude Delamire would be mentioned. It rarely was, unless Robin introduced it himself, which he sometimes did at the fag-end of the evening, in a shy yet off-hand fashion, as though she were to him merely one of fifty, instead of the bright particular angel of his thoughts and dreams. He was sympathetic, too, in the way in which he acquiesced in David's encomiums, in the hope of wringing a favorable opinion from him in regard to her. But David was obdurate, if he understood, or more probably simply indifferent. When once he was brought to bay by a direct question from Robin, he answered:

"Oh, yes, she is well enough. A pretty little thing, but too thin for my style. Compare her with Edith Harris, for instance. There's a neck and pair of shoulders for you! I like women with go, who speak up."

"Yes," said Robin. The very fact of having breathed her name aloud had brought the color to his cheeks. He was grateful for being able to talk about her, even though the outcome was so meagre. "Miss Delamire looks better at some times than others," he added, almost apologetically, and he blushed again.

"I dare say. Oh, she's well enough," responded Finn, carelessly.

Gertrude Delamire was just the sort of girl whom a sensitive discerning man would fall in love with. She was as delicate as a Sèvres china cup, alike in physique and thought; but she possessed the delicacy of strength, not of decay. It was natural enough that David Finn should accuse her of not speaking up, for she was dainty in her speech and bearing, and never did the wooing. I remember well how sweet she looked on the afternoon when our bachelor house was opened for a tea that spring—one of Robin's happy suggestions, of which even old Dodd approved. The refreshments were served in Finn's room, but she lingered below to examine a second time the sketch from the Gorner Grat which hung on Richard Benton's wall. Robin was on the way upstairs, and I heard Miss Edith Harris exclaim to him, " Your rooms are too lovely for anything, Mr. Temple, and this is such fun," which was the same remark she had made a moment before to me.

" Isn't that delightful ? " I said, addressing Miss Delamire from the doorway. She seemed to start at my question, for she had apparently supposed herself alone. " So full of poetry and feeling," I added.

" Oh yes," she said, fervently ; only that, and our eyes met ; but hers fell, and I had guessed her secret. Robin Temple had won her gentle heart.

During that spring David Finn and Robin were much together, and were often to be seen side by side on the former's cart. I said to Finn once, by way of expressing mildly my surprise, though I had to conceal my disapprobation, " What, if you'll excuse an impudent question, is it that you and Robin Temple find in common?"

"Do you know, Uncle George," was the jaunty answer, as though he were announcing a discovery, " Robin's not half a bad lot. I thought at first there was a good deal of the sissy about him, but that's only because he's a little different from the rest of us. They call it the artistic temperament, don't they? Well, all I can say is, I'd give ducats if I could tie a necktie as he does. On my word, clothes which he has worn a year, and bought ready-made to begin with, fit him better than my things from Poole fit me. If he'd only get rid of the idea that he can make his living by painting pictures, and settle down to something practical, I believe he'd go ahead fast. I've told him so half a dozen times. He was a fool to let that partnership slip. Why don't you say a word to him, Dodd, on the same lay? Somehow I think he'd take it better from you. Well, ta-ta."

We had reached the corner where our ways separated, but I reached out my hand and detained him.

"See here, Finn," said I, "if you're really

SHE LINGERED BELOW TO EXAMINE THE SKETCH

a friend of Robin Temple's, you'll stop saying anything of the kind to him."

"What do you mean?"

"His art is his salvation."

"Art with a capital A?" he asked, with an amused grin.

"I don't understand you," I answered, coldly. "He has very unusual talent. It may be some time before it is appreciated so that he is able to sell his pictures to advantage, but if he perseveres he is not unlikely, in my judgment, to become one of the foremost artists of the world." I spoke gravely.

Finn looked at me for a moment with a half-quizzical, half-scornful air. I could see that he was not convinced.

"The best thing for him to do, then, is to marry a rich wife, isn't it?" he asked, with an effort to treat the matter lightly.

"I am sure," I said, "that Robin Temple will never marry any woman for her money, even if it were suggested to him."

Finn was not an easy man to offend, and my rudeness seemed merely to imply to him a lack of humor on my part. He put out his hand, and patting me patronizingly on the shoulder, said, with a knowing laugh : "It isn't out of the bounds of possibility, is it, Uncle George, that a man might be in love with two women at the same time, and be influenced in his final choice by the fact that one had money and the other was poor as a church mouse? If he were to marry the rich one, could anyone say that he was marrying her for her money? Now think that over, Uncle George, when you've nothing to do, and let me know," he added with a buoyant chuckle, and strode away.

Robin's first exhibition was in the following October. He displayed twelve pictures in the gallery of a prominent dealer. It was on the second day that Richard burst into my room bubbling over with the announcement that two had already been sold, in addition to the one which he himself had picked out to own. "The critics are with us, too," he added. "There was a first-rate notice in this morning's *Despatch ;* and Brummel, who usually tries to crush the life out of beginners, happened in while I was there, and volunteered to tell me that he should give them a send-off in the *Mercury.*"

I was not able to pay my respects to the exhibition until the following day. I had

seen most of the pictures in process of com-
position, so that I had a general idea of their
excellence, but as I viewed them completed
and as a whole, I was even more pleased
than I had expected to be. I chose a bright
landscape—a bit of woodland and river—
which seemed to me thoroughly spirited.
On leaving the exhibition gallery one had to
pass into the main store, and as I dallied for
a moment to examine the dealer's treasures,
Miss Gertrude Delamire came in from the
street, without noticing me, I think. She
hesitated an instant, then made some inquiries about a frame in what seemed to me
a timid, abashed manner. I pretended to be
very busy admiring the lines of one of
Barye's lions, and slipped out presently into
the street without obtruding my personality
on her maiden fancy.

The exhibition lasted ten days, and of the
twelve pictures six were sold ; three of them
to people unknown to Robin. Eight hundred dollars, less the dealer's commission,
was the net return, which seemed to our
young artist a prosperous beginning. He
informed Finn of his good fortune on the
evening after the exhibition closed, as they

sat smoking in my room. I think Robin was a little nettled that David had not taken the trouble to look in during the ten days, for though he said nothing definite, there was a slight tremor of reproach in the tone in which he remarked,

"I took in eight hundred dollars clean money, and sold half my pictures."

The idea that he had been remiss was evidently in Finn's mind too, for he said, presently : "The market has been feverish this week, and I've been busy. I meant to have a squint at them, Robin, but somehow the time passed, and I didn't get round to it."

"That's all right," replied Robin. "You've seen most of them first or last lying about my room."

David said nothing for a moment. An idea had occurred to him, and presently he gave us the benefit of it. "I suppose, Robin, you'd be ready to sell the other six for the same amount of money? Well, now, I tell you what : I'll match you heads or tails to see whether they belong to me, or I pay you another eight hundred dollars. Pictures are not much in my line, barring the great masters, but Uncle George here says you

may be a big bug one of these days, and if
so, I shall be getting in on the ground-floor.
Is it a gamble ? ”

I could have shaken Finn, though I dare
say he imagined that he was making a generous proposal.

Robin flushed at first at the careless words
and bantering tone, but I could see that on
second thought he was fascinated. He glanced
at me as though for my approval.

“ This isn’t the Stock Exchange, Finn,” I
exclaimed.

“ No ; but I’ve made a square offer, which
I’m ready to stand by.”

“ I’ll do it,” said Robin, suddenly.

“ Very well. Uncle George, will you
manipulate the coin ? You may name it,
Robin.”

I drew reluctantly from my pocket the
necessary half - dollar, and spun it into the
air. Robin won.

Finn instantly took out his pocket-book.
“ I’ll draw you a check now,” he said, and
he was proceeding to do so, when he suddenly laid down the pen. “ What do you
say, Robin, to my buying you a hundred
shares of Atchison with this ? It’s going up.

13

I'd almost be willing to guarantee you against loss."

Robin's eyes gleamed furtively. "I don't know anything about such things. How much would I make?"

"If I put it up as a margin you ought to make another thousand beside the eight hundred."

"Or lose the eight hundred," I interjected.

This must have piqued Finn, for he retorted, boldly: "Come, now, I'd like to see you make some money. I *will* guarantee you against loss. And you too, Uncle George, if you'd like to take a flier."

"Thanks—no; I never speculate," I answered.

Robin looked at us both. "I'd be glad to make some money, if you can make it for me," he replied, eagerly.

"Enough said," said Finn.

When another autumn came round Robin had a new lot of pictures to exhibit. Again the critics were highly complimentary, though not so unreservedly so as on the first occasion. They asserted the critic's prerogative to point out what they thought the strong and weak points in his art. They evidently regarded him no longer as a beginner, but an artist of recognized standing. Seven pictures out of sixteen were sold, at a slight advance in price. Both to Richard Benton and to me this result seemed very satisfactory; and we felt that Robin had made progress—that his fancy was bolder and his technique more perfect. During this time his attentions to Miss Delamire had become conspicuous, and I knew from various enigmatic speeches which he let fall from month to month that he was anxious to marry her. He was, comparatively speaking, in funds at this time, for Finn had sent him a check for eighteen hundred dollars in less than six weeks from the time of their conversation. I fancy that Robin made use of much of this for flowers for Miss Delamire, and in trying to keep pace with her other admirers in the gay world. I could see that he was restless, and he became more so after David Finn's engagement to Miss Edith Harris was announced, and that prosperous couple were to be seen daily on a brand-new black and yellow cart behind the well-groomed cob.

"Confound it all, Dodd," said he to me one evening, "how is an artist to marry?"

"On nothing," I answered, promptly.

I felt sure that though he had heard me rail at times against improvident marriages, and the cruelty of bringing children into the world to struggle with well-bred poverty, he would not misunderstand me. I knew that the vision of Miss Edith Harris in perpetually superb attire, with a mass of roses at her waist, and mistress of a magnificent establishment, haunted his mind's eye, and would not down at the bidding. He turned the conversation, and studied the fire almost in silence for an hour after; but when he rose at last to leave me he pressed my hand and said :

"I'm going to make a new departure. I'm going to paint a face—an ideal, not a portrait. It will be the best thing I have done. The old masters did Madonnas of the skies, but the world of to-day is inspired by noble earthly women."

Finn was married in the spring, and our house knew him no more. He had built himself an elaborate house in town, another at the seaside, and was apparently on the top of the wave. I was secretly delighted at his exodus, for I felt convinced that Robin would be able to work less interruptedly. My astonishment and consternation, therefore, were great when, the following autumn, about the time another exhibition by Robin was due, Richard Benton came into my room one evening and said:

"Temple is going into business. The coffee business," he added, in response to my ejaculations of dismay. "His brother has given him another chance, as he calls it, and he has accepted it. I have been talking with him for two hours, but he is adamant. He says he wishes to be married, and that he must make money. I reasoned with him, but it was of no use. He says he will be able to paint in his leisure moments and vacations. You know what that means. He has fallen down and worshipped the golden calf. The devil take that fellow Finn and all his tribe!"

"Amen!" I muttered.

"He is throwing himself away. There is not one man in a million with his talent, and he is going into the coffee business. Pshaw! Robin, Robin, you have played us false!"

High as my opinion was of Richard Benton, the fervor of his disappointment was a

surprise to me. I did not insult his manly
intelligence by pretending to palliate the
matter. We turned it over in every light,
and I promised to see Robin on the morrow
and add my remonstrances to those of his
best friend, though I felt convinced that they
would be made in vain.

Robin evidently expected me. He was
standing on the hearth-rug, and when he saw
who his visitor was, his expression indicated
a harassed soul at bay. He did not suggest
my sitting down, and when I had established
myself nonchalantly in an arm-chair and
lighted a pipe, he said, with nervous deci-
siveness :

"I know why you have come, Uncle George.
But it's of no use. I've made up my mind,
and nothing anyone can say will change it."

Accordingly I talked of other things, and
presently, with the familiarity of one accustomed to take liberties there, I strolled over
to his easel and lifted the covering. A face
looked back at me—a face only half completed, and yet already so excellent, so original in conception and treatment, that I
stepped back eagerly to scan it. A woman's
face. Where had I seen it? Yet the cos-

A FACE LOOKED BACK AT ME

tume and surroundings indicated that it was a study in fancy rather than a portrait. Then I recalled our conversation of six months before, and understood. But the likeness? There was no likeness, after all; but I understood, too, whose face had served as an inspiration to the artist.

"Robin," I exclaimed, earnestly, "this is superb. It far surpasses anything you have done before."

He smiled coldly. "Thanks. I am glad you like it. I shall try to finish it some day." Then he walked up to the easel and replaced the covering.

I appreciated the definiteness of the hint, but I could not restrain myself.

"Robin," I said, "how will the woman whose soul looks from those eyes like what you are doing?"

He started as though I had struck him—and, indeed, it was an impertinence; but are not the wounds of friendship faithful?—and the blood surged to his face. He stared at me haughtily.

"I do not understand what you mean," he said. "What right have you to pry into my affairs?"

"Only because I love you, Robin," I said, gently, and left him.

There was from this time a coolness, almost a breach, between us, though we still paid occasional visits to each other's rooms, and preserved the outward show of amity. Robin went into business, and a year and a half slipped away without any apparent change in his or my circumstances. He came and went like any young man who is occupied down-town, and as our intimacy had been inter-rupted, he was mute in my presence as to his private affairs. I understood, however, that he was early and late at the office.

It was at the end of the second spring after Robin abandoned art that I went abroad, in consequence of the demolition of our lodg-ing-house, preparatory to the erection of the imposing Rexford. Like the very rats, forced after a long and fond occupation to seek shelter elsewhere, we fled right and left, ac-cording to our moods and necessities. Rich-ard and Robin sought a haven in one of the other bachelor warrens in the same neighbor-hood, and I stored my penates, packed my portmanteau, and took the first steamer to Europe. There I remained two years—a little longer, in fact, for I did not return until the snow was on the ground, and the plaster of the Rexford was thoroughly dry, and its modern improvements in complete working order. I had arranged to have my penates re-established in my new quarters, so that I might walk in on a furnished apartment almost as though I had not been away. I arrived late in the evening, to find a fire on the hearth, a bit of supper on the table, and the evening *Mercury* at my elbow. Being fresh from the steamer, I was in arrears regarding events, and after my appetite was satisfied I was soon deep in local news. I turned first to the financial page to ascertain the standing of my few securities. Somehow it comforts or depresses a man, as the case may be, to know that the stock he owns is five points higher or lower, though he has not the least idea of selling it in either event. Speculation was running riot, it seemed to me, and the rumors of the day prophesied that the advance had only just begun. Having ascertained that I was considerably richer on paper, I turned to the marriages and deaths, and as I read, I stopped to read again, struck with horror :

"In this city, on December the 6th, Robert Temple, in the thirtieth year of his age. Funeral at St. Mark's Church, on Tuesday, December 10th, at one o'clock."

Robin Temple dead, and his funeral to-morrow! I pressed the electric button, and the new janitor, who had served my supper, appeared. "I see the announcement of Mr. Robert Temple's death?" I said, interrogatively.

"Yes, sir. He died day before yesterday, of pneumonia, and he's to be buried to-morrow. He had rooms here, sir."

I had not known, though I had supposed it might be so. "Here, in this apartment-house?"

"Yes, sir. I thought of speaking about it, but I wasn't sure you knew him, and I wouldn't mention it until you'd had your supper."

"Thank you, Perkins," I said, to acknowledge consideration so unusual. "Yes, I knew him well. Of pneumonia?"

"He was taken ill a week ago Sunday, sir; and there were three doctors at the last, and Mr. Benton, besides the nurse, was with him night and day," added Perkins, with the fluency of one who feels that he is free at last to tell all he knows.

"Mr. Richard Benton?"

"Yes, sir. He came in just before you rang. He's grieving sadly, sir."

"Please go and tell Mr. Benton that I am coming down to see him."

Five minutes later I stood with Richard beside the open coffin and looked at our friend as he lay in the sleep of death. The fell disease had left few traces, and even the unconquerable enemy had laid only the seal of marble-like pallor upon the likeness of our Robin. The poet-like eyes were closed, but the dainty features, the delicate contour of brow and lip and chin, were still the same. He was there, yet he was gone— gone to the land of mystery, from which none return to tell of the mercies of God's judgment-seat.

As I looked around me presently, when I had turned away from the coffin, I noticed that the new rooms, into which he had moved only two months before, were exquisitely furnished; but there was only a single suggestion of the artist's craft—an easel in one corner, over which an Eastern cloth had been thrown. Somehow I divined what was beneath, and, impelled by the desire to ascertain, I crossed the room and raised the covering. The same face, fixed by a master's hand, yet unfinished and unaltered, looked out at me from the canvas. Apparently he had never touched it with his brush since our interview two years before.

I heard from Richard's lips that night all that he knew. " He worked like a slave, Dodd; down early and up late. About a year ago his brother died, and the other partner was called to California by the illness of his wife, and Robin's opportunity, as he thought, had come. The coffee market was depressed, unduly so, and he bought, and bought again, borrowing heavily. He was right. In ninety days the tide had turned, and he had made over two hundred thousand dollars. He told me this four months ago, and he has died rich, for so young a man. He seemed exultantly happy, and his manner of living changed at once. He bought a stylish turn-out, and he fitted up these rooms ; though he said to me, poor fellow, with a knowing smile, the day he moved into them, ' I may not need them very long.' Ten days ago I was sitting in my room late. It was a brutal night—cold, with a piercing wind, and the streets a glare of frozen sleet. I had been beguiled into sitting up—it was nearly two—by a new book, which I had just finished, when there came a knock at the door, and Robin staggered in; it was just that—staggered. He was pale and distract-ed-looking. His overcoat—not a heavy one—was unbuttoned, and his evening dress awry, as though blown by the wind. He sank into a chair and covered his face with his hands. 'My God, Robin, what is the matter?' I asked. He looked up at me with an expression of agony I shall never forget, and answered, in a piteous voice, 'She has refused me, Richard, and my heart is broken.' It seems he had been walking the streets in that guise for hours. I watched over him that night. He was ill already, and the next morning he was in a high fever. We did all we could, but he died day before yesterday."

The following afternoon we laid Robin's body in the grave. It was a brilliant win-ter's day. The landscape revealed, even to the common eye, the subtle hues which ar-tists love. Richard and I drove back from the cemetery together. He had been silent for a time, but as we were nearing home he suddenly said : "How little money can avail, after all ! I am worth to-day half a million dollars, Dodd. How gladly would I give Robin the half of it—which is what he will leave behind him—if one could wipe out the last five years, and put him back at his easel just as he once was! But that is all over and past forever."

It was not quite so. As I have stated, those were days of rampant speculation. But, as is apt to be the case, the crash came suddenly and without apparent warning. Many went to the wall, and rumor, which had whispered a month ago that the advance had only just begun, now prophesied that there would be worse failures after the first of the year. It was on Christmas-eve, I remember, that I went down to Richard Benton's room and found David Finn there. My visit was purely a casual one. Perhaps the cockles of my heart were oppressed with the sense of loneliness which an old bachelor is apt to experience at this season. As I entered I perceived from their faces that I had interrupted the discussion of some serious matter, and was closing the door, when I was restrained by Richard's voice saying, "Come back, Dodd; you shall be the judge."

I turned back in response to this summons, wondering, and Richard waved me to a seat. Finn was standing, with his back to the fireplace. I noticed, in the few moments of silence which followed, that he looked worried, though his old air of confidence had not forsaken him.

"Dodd," said Richard again, "you shall be the judge between us." Then he addressed Finn: "You have come to me to-night and told me that you are in trouble. You have asked me, as a director of the bank where your largest loans are placed, to consent to their renewal, and I have told you that I cannot. My duty as an officer forbids that; we cannot take the risk. I told you this, and you have just asked me to help you as an individual. I might do so if I chose. I have some means, and I could tide you over; and coming as you do at this Christmas-time, I would tide you over but for one thing, and Uncle George here shall decide if I am not right. If he says that I am unjust, my credit shall be at your disposal."

For an instant he paused, and I could see that Finn was groping for the reason. He had no inkling of it, though I felt sure that I knew.

"But for you and men like you, my friend Robin Temple would not be in his grave. You and your example fascinated him until he prostituted the noble gift which God had given him. Day in, day out, he heard you sneer at everything which did not stand for money and the coarse or showy gratifications which mere money can purchase. He learned from you to sacrifice everything for that, and awoke at last to know the agony and bitterness of his delusion. It killed him. He was my dearest friend. You have asked me to help you. My answer is, I refuse you in the name of Robin Temple. Let Dodd, who knows the truth, judge between us."

In spite of the death-blow which these words gave to Finn's hopes, and though he winced a little, a smile curved his lip, recalling vividly his look on the day when he had queried, in answer to my declaration that Robin's art was his salvation, "Art with a capital A?" The same flippant, cruel smile, as though the speech had amused him by its somewhat dramatic intensity. Then, as I looked at him, there came into my mind the words of the Psalmist—" The fool hath said in his heart, There is no God."

" Finn," I said, " my judgment is that Richard is right."

" Oh, very well. This is absurd," said Finn. " I am no more responsible for the death of Robin Temple than either one of you." There was a brief silence, during which he made his preparations for departure. " It strikes me," he added, bitterly, as he buttoned his overcoat, " that you have scarcely looked at this matter in a business-like manner."

" No," said Richard, quietly. " It is purely a matter of sentiment."

Ten days later—just after the 1st of January—the suspension of David Finn & Company, bankers and brokers, was announced in the newspapers in startling head-lines, and before another eighteen months had passed I acted as best man to Richard Benton on the occasion of his marriage to Gertrude Delamire.

THE MATRIMONIAL TONTINE
BENEFIT ASSOCIATION

THE MATRIMONIAL TONTINE
BENEFIT ASSOCIATION

THE Matrimonial Tontine Mutual Benefit Association of New York was reduced to two members. These were Benjamin Davis, note broker, and Horace Wilson,
landscape gardener. The rest were married
or buried. That is to say, one member, poor
Thomas Cook, was under the sod, and the
other twelve were Benedicks in good standing. There had not been even a divorce,
though divorce was not a contingency provided for in the constitution.

The Association was twelve years old, and
owed its existence to a random remark made
by Harry Stephenson at a dinner at the
club.

" I wonder," said he, " which of us fellows
will marry first."

" Or last," said Ben Davis.

" Or not at all," said Horace Wilson.

There was some lively banter on the subject, chiefly to the effect that marriage as an institution was decaying, and that no one but a Crœsus could afford to take a wife, and presently George Edmunds, who had been smoking reflectively, drew general attention to himself by rapping on the table.

" I have a scheme to propose," he said.

George Edmunds was known to have a nimble fancy and to be a practical individual into the bargain. He was a writer of fiction, but he had invented in his spare moments a patent corkscrew and a patent potato-peeler which brought him in a round sum annually. Consequently any scheme of his suggestion was sure to be listened to respectfully.

"There are fifteen of us here to-night," he continued, "and there can't be a difference of two years between the eldest and the youngest. Why shouldn't we form a Bachelors' Protective Union ? "

He paused and looked round the room inquiringly. Several smiled as though the idea pleased them; but evidently no one knew exactly what George meant; and by way of inviting elucidation, Ben Davis, who probably had the potato-peeler in mind, asked :

"Where's the chance for making an honest dollar this time?"

"I'll show you," replied George. "Fifteen members at an annual assessment of twenty-five dollars apiece will insure a dinner on the first of every January for the party, and leave a neat little annual sum to be invested by the treasurer. The last man who holds out against the enemy takes the pool. If the fund is skilfully handled, and we hold out as rigorously as we talk, he ought to carry off a tidy sum."

There was a murmur of approval and amusement.

"It's a pious plan," exclaimed Stephenson. "Let's put it through."

"We will," said several others.

"But suppose there never should be a last man? There might be several, you know, who would hold out to the end," said Ben Davis. "There should be a time limit when the survivors divide."

This seemed sensible, and it was subsequently agreed that at the end of twenty years the pool should be apportioned in case there should be more than a single bachelor remaining.

Before midnight on that very evening the articles of association were drawn up by the flowing pen of George Edmunds, and read to the assembled company. There was a preamble with a formidable *Whereas.* " *Whereas* we, the undersigned bachelors, have this day entered into a solemn compact for the mutual protection of our liberties against the institution of marriage, etc., etc." Then followed a solemn bond wherein The Matrimonial Tontine Mutual Benefit Association of New York bound itself, in consideration of certain covenants and agreements of each subscriber, to furnish a dinner of reasonable richness as to food, and abundance as to drink, on the first day of each and every year, and to pay over to the individual or individuals who should be most faithful to the purposes of the Association the total net capital accumulated from the time of the first payment down to the date of the final settlement.

Everybody signed that night, and there was much flamboyant protestation on the subject of matrimony. To judge merely from the expressed views of the subscribers, it seemed probable that the pool would be divided among the fifteen members at the end of the twenty years. The average age of the subscribers was twenty-five. No one was over twenty-six or under twenty-four. Consequently the limit of twenty years appeared to be a reasonable one. Surely a bachelor of forty-five ought to be able to take care of himself, and do without the protection of a Bachelors' Union.

The subscribers, having duly affixed their signatures to the articles of association, elected, as seemed fitting, George Edmunds president, secretary, and treasurer. It would be his duty to call the members together on the occasion of the annual dinner, to note and report failures to pay the annual dues or fallings from grace into matrimony, to exercise general supervision over the affairs of the Association, and particular supervision over the net fund. He was given, by the oral instructions of the members, plenary and yet peculiar and sleep-haunting powers as to the management of this fund. No gilt-edged conventional investment returning regular, modest interest would satisfy the winner of the pool. The treasurer would be expected

to hit upon something extraordinary in its
dividend-yielding character. If not another
potato-peeler, something equally bonanza-
like and gratifying. And yet no risks must
be run which would hazard the integrity of
the principal. Something safe yet unconventional, perfectly secure but splendidly
lucrative, would be expected from him.
George would understand what they meant
and act accordingly, and doubtless the event-
ual winner of the pool would have every reason to approve of their selection of a treasurer.

Whether it be that much of the talk this
evening was on the surface and merely for
effect or bravado, or whether it be that the
masculine heart may contain matrimonial
germs without being conscious of them, no
less than four of the fifteen subscribers ceased
to be members of the Association after paying but two annual assessments—that is to
say, they became engaged in the course of
the second year. A summer girl at Narragansett Pier caused the first break, which
was the occasion of an extra dinner and much
oratory as to the necessity of caution and
steadfastness. Within the three ensuing
months, thereby suggesting that the deserters

probably had matrimony in their minds at the time these speeches of exhortation were being made, a second, third, and fourth fell victims to a widow with two children, a flaxen-haired doll, and a strong-minded brunette, respectively. So the women in question were stigmatized by the remaining members, who closed up their serried ranks and looked askance at one another. *Who* would be the next to fall? Who, indeed! But there was always the consolation that the individual chances of the survivors to win the pool had been materially enhanced. As for the pool itself, the treasurer had already doubled it by a happy purchase of some shares in a gold mine.

During the next two years there was no lapse from grace, and simply the death of Tom Cook to chronicle. Then, without warning, Harry Stephenson came a fearful cropper, as they say in the hunting-field. He fell over head and ears in love with a very plain girl in Harlem, without a penny to her name, and married her. This made a frightful gap, for Harry had been one of the most inspiring and virulent bachelors of the Association. What was more, his defection seemed to knock the moral fortitude out of William Hardy, so that when the fifth annual dinner came round, only eight members clinked their glasses and drank a standing toast to the joys and blessings of single life. On the following day, one of the eight announced his engagement to a chit of eighteen. This bit of perfidy elicited from the survivors a special vote of censure which accompanied the box of flowers sent by them to the victimizer of their late associate. The only cheering bit of intelligence was, that the treasurer had again done his duty. He had sold the shares of the gold mine at a magnificent figure, and put them into the stock of the Oleo Refrigerator Company, which had immediately declared a cash dividend of fifty per cent.

After this there was another lull of two years and a half. Then, at intervals of about six months apart, three more fell from grace, leaving only George Edmunds, Benjamin Davis, Horace Wilson, and Roger Partridge to dine together on the occasion of the tenth annual dinner. Partridge, who was bald-headed and looked like a confirmed old bachelor of the first water, was nevertheless so melancholy and absent‑minded that the president, secretary, and treasurer called him to order and directed the eyes of the Association upon him so sharply that the poor fellow blushed to where roots of his hair had been.

“You had better confess and make a clean breast of it,” said Ben Davis.

“I've nothing to confess,” answered Partridge, stoutly. But he looked exceedingly doleful, and of a sudden he collapsed and blurted out, “I offered myself to a woman yesterday and she threw me over. If that's a reason for resigning, I'll resign. I wish somebody would blow my brains out.” Thereupon he buried his head in his hands.

There was a short silence, and the other three exchanged sardonic glances.

“Does the constitution cover the case?” asked Ben Davis.

“No. The repentant sinner is received back with open arms,” said Edmunds. “Cheer up, Roger. You've run a frightful risk, but you still have a grip on the pool, dear boy. Only don't ask her again.”

“She wouldn't have me if I did,” groaned the culprit.

"Oh, yes, she would."

"What makes you think so?" eagerly asked the bald-headed bachelor.

"Because in nine cases out of ten they do."

"Then you think I'd have a chance?"

"What's her age, old fellow, if she'll excuse the question?"

"Twenty-nine next August."

"It's nearly a dead certainty," exclaimed Edmunds and Davis, in the same breath.

"My opinion is that if you don't ask her, she'll ask you," said Horace Wilson.

This was a little brutal. Horace, who really had a tender heart, felt it to be so. He put his hand gently on Roger's shoulder.

"I say," he exclaimed a moment later, "this thing has gone far enough. Fate is against the Association. I vote that we disband."

"Disband!" cried Davis. "That is a monstrous idea. What do you mean?"

On the other hand, Edmunds made no such demonstration of protest. Indeed, a careful observer would have noticed that a flicker of satisfaction passed across his countenance. But all he said was—he said it, though, a

THE TENTH ANNUAL DINNER—" SHE THREW ME OVER "

little nervously—" We four should get about fifteen hundred apiece. The fund figures a trifle more than six thousand on my books to-day."

"Money or no money," said Horace, "we've carried it far enough. We have vindicated our principles; we are each of us thirty-five, and now it seems to me that any-one of us ought to be allowed to marry without loss of self-respect."

"There is certainly something in what you say," said Edmunds, with an appearance of dispassionate candor.

Davis gazed from one to the other in mingled astonishment and indignation. "I never heard such a thing," he exclaimed. "Disband just when we're reaching the crucial point! It's the brassiest proposition I ever listened to. Even Roger, here, who would get his fifteen hundred by it, looks as though he thought it the most extraordinary idea that was ever broached. I see through it, though," he continued, defiantly. "It's a conspiracy. You two are either engaged or in love, and have put your heads together to play me for an imbecile. But it won't work. The Association can't disband without a unanimous vote, and mine is not to be had for love or money. Come now, George Edmunds and Horace Wilson, admit that you're in love and that this is a game. You can't look me straight in the eyes, George. By Jove, you're the most conscious-looking conspirator who was ever brought to bay."

Undeniably, Edmunds, from the moment this accusation was uttered, had worn a flurried air, and now, when Davis seized him by the arms and tried to look into his eyes, he winced and avoided the searching, scornful scrutiny, and turned pink and white. Even his would-be nonchalant words of protest did not clinch the matter, as his accuser was quick to discover.

"Engaged? Nonsense. I never asked a woman to marry me in my life."

"But you're in love. Deny it if you can."

"I deny your right—" began George. "Er —besides it's not true."

"I knew it," cried Ben, triumphantly, and, letting Edmunds loose, he bent his gaze on Horace Wilson. "And here's another in the same fix."

This time there was no wincing or shrinking. The scornful, piercing eyes encountered a cool, steady return, and there was the resonance of convincing truth in the sturdy reply:

"Ben Davis, unless we disband to-night, you, barring my death, will never touch one dollar of that six thousand until the end of the twenty years, and then you will have to divide it with me. Conspiracy? There isn't a woman in this world whom I would cross the street to speak to a second time. And more's the pity, too. What I said about disbanding came from my heart. Heaven knows I'd like to fall in love, but I can't. I've tried, but it's no use. If there ever was a firm-set old bachelor, I'm the man; and since you decline to disband, I warn you to look out, for I intend to take the pool."

Thereupon Horace folded his arms and smiled with the assurance of a man who has been many times under fire and still is heart-whole.

You will remember that this occurred at the tenth annual dinner. Before the eleventh Roger Partridge offered himself again and was accepted. The remaining three dined together on the first of January, and clinked their glasses once more to perpetual bachelor-

15

hood. Although George Edmunds made no formal announcement, his undisguised attentions to Miss Virginia Tebbetts, and her apparent preference for him, left little room to doubt that his membership in the Association hung by the gills, so to speak, and that the contest was to be limited to the other two. Indeed, Ben Davis felt that the president, secretary, and treasurer was so completely out of the race that he saw fit, in the spirit of prudence which was an attribute of his, to throw out a hint or two as to the advisability of conservatism in regard to the investment of the pool. The treasurer had again made a notable financial stroke by selling out the stock of the "Oleo Refrigerator Company" at the top of the market, and buying the shares of the "Plimsoll Aëronautic Concern" at a bed-rock price.

"Don't you think it might be well to salt down what we have into a first-rate real-estate mortgage?" inquired Ben.

George Edmunds flushed. He was not prone to take offence, but he prided himself on his acumen as an investor, and this remark seemed to him to savor of rank ingratitude and to be entirely uncalled for.

“Haven't I done sufficiently well for you?” he replied.

“You have done wonders — made three ten-strokes; but—but I think you will admit that there was a certain element of risk in each one of the—er—investments.”

“They succeeded,” said George, coldly.

“Besides, the treasurer was directed to be brilliant,” interjected Horace. “There is no scope for brilliancy in a first-rate real-estate mortgage.”

“That was at first, when we had a mere pittance in the treasury. We have ten thousand dollars now. Ten thousand dollars does not grow on every bush, but it may be lost in a twinkling. What if the flying-machine does not work? Where will our money be?”

Undoubtedly George Edmunds laid up this criticism against Ben so far as a kind-hearted and malice-hating fellow could lay up anything against anybody. This, too, in spite of the fact that the stock of the “Plimsoll Aëronautic Concern” rose rapidly during the next four months, demonstrating clearly thereby the superior sagacity of the treasurer of the Matrimonial Tontine Mutual

Benefit Association. At a special meeting of the members, held on the first day of May, this self-same treasurer announced, with the apologetic reprehension of self which the fall of the chief and sole official of the Association seemed to demand, his engagement to Miss Virginia Tebbetts.

"I have called a special meeting," he continued, "for the reason that, as I have ceased to be a member, a new custodian of the assets of the Association should be elected forthwith. The only present asset is this certificate for one thousand shares of the stock of the 'Plimsoll Aëronautic Concern,' which I take pleasure in informing you could be sold to-day for twelve thousand five hundred dollars."

Thereupon, with a glance of legitimate triumph at Ben Davis, he laid the valuable piece of parchment on the table, together with the records of the Association, and presently left the two survivors to their own devices.

On the following morning, before a single quotation was uttered in Wall Street, Ben Davis entered a broker's office with the piece of parchment in question, duly endorsed by him as president, secretary, and treasurer of the Association.

"Sell this at the market," he said, carelessly. But though he looked cool as a cucumber, there was fever in his soul, and he hung about the office until the operation was completed. The stock was sold for $12,500, and the following week it fell $5 a share in as many minutes, and within a fortnight the certificates were worth merely what old paper is worth. But long before that dismal day the funds of the Matrimonial Tontine Mutual Benefit Association were safely invested in a gilt-edged mortgage on improved real estate.

And so, as was stated in the first place, the Association was reduced to two members, a condition of affairs which had existed now for three calendar years. The fourteenth annual dinner had recently been eaten, and Ben Davis and Horace Wilson had clinked glasses to the joys of single life with the same gusto, so far as either could discern by close scrutiny of the other, displayed by them on the very first occasion. Beyond the fact that George Edmunds had been married and was the father of a boy baby, and the funds of the Association were yielding a safe but modest four and one-half per cent., matters seemed just the same. But they were not.

One winter's evening, about six weeks subsequent to the fourteenth annual dinner, Ben Davis sat before the fire in his comfortable bachelor rooms, with a pensive expression of countenance. Time had dealt kindly with Ben. He had some hair left, a moderately youthful face and figure, and a prosperous business. People and corporations who were pressed for money came to him to relieve their necessities, and he was very apt to be able to relieve them. When he did so, he retained a small slice ; such is the way of the world ; and it does not take a very great many slices to make a respectable family loaf. But Ben had no family. He kept a cob, and he went to Europe for six weeks in summer, provided the money market was not too tight. In the event of financial stringency he ran down to Bar Harbor for a fortnight or so. Money had been at a premium the previous summer, and he had been able to get away only for ten days, and to get only as far as Narragansett Pier. But those ten days had been detrimental to his peace of mind ever since.   He had seen her in the water the first time, and he could not forget her.

She did not live in New York ; but such are the opportunities of a note broker that one can run over to Philadelphia on business without seeming to go out of one's way to call on a girl. Ben had made the trip five times since the first of October, and it was not yet March, and he had fairly come to the conclusion that single life was a failure. What he was saying to himself this evening was that on Easter he would send her a lily, and go over the following week and ask her to become his. In the event that she accepted him, Horace Wilson, of course, would get the money. This was not exactly a pleasant thought for Ben; but so far as he could see, there would be no escape from it. Somehow he had come to regard the pool as his, and the idea of losing it entirely was galling. Not that he needed the money; for he was doing remarkably well. Indeed, the sum would make a much greater difference to Horace Wilson than to him, for Horace, though described in common parlance as a rising landscape gardener, had only half his income. It would certainly be unpleasant, though, to be obliged to take the little trunk out from the safe and hand it over to Horace. The gilt-edged mortgage on improved real estate seemed to him to belong just where it was, and the prospect of parting with it was very distasteful to him. Was there no means by which he could win her and the pool both?

None presented itself that evening, but on the following morning, which was Sunday, he stumbled upon something just a little promising. Up to this time during the last five years he had never seen Horace Wilson in the society of any woman. Though the city was large, to be sure, and they did not meet altogether the same people, Ben flattered himself that he kept a pretty close eye on Horace. And yet the painful consciousness was his that never had he run across his rival in what might be called a compromising situation. Had he detected him even at a theatre-party, he would have felt encouraged, but though he had often beheld Horace comfortably ensconced in an orchestra stall, there had never been a female companion beside him.

On this Sunday morning, however, as Ben was taking an airing, chance led him along the particular cross street in which George Edmunds had established his household gods. The churches were just out, and though it was a cross street, there was a sprinkling of people on either sidewalk. Ben was thinking of her, and consequently did not pay his customary heed to the passers. There was only one woman in the world for him, and as for the men, they interested him not at all, provided the single ones stayed away from Philadelphia. There was just one man he would except from the general scope of his indifference, and he was Horace Wilson. Why the dickens didn't that fellow get married? It was high time. Happening to look across the street as this thought formulated itself in his mind, his heart gave a jump. In the vestibule of George Edmunds's house stood four people, who were on the point of entering. Indeed, before he had fully comprehended the situation, they had gone in and shut the door. But in three of them Ben had recognized George and his wife and Horace Wilson. As to the fourth, who had been slightly in advance of the others, and consequently partially concealed, he had detected by the feathers on her bonnet that she was a

woman, and a passably young woman at that.
Ben, being a note broker, was quick at com-
putation. He instantly put two and two together and said to himself that Horace had
been escorting the unknown in question home
from church. A ray of hope lit up his late
gloomy reflections regarding the gilt-edged
mortgage. If Horace were to become engaged before he did, the pool would be his.
After glancing up at the house opposite in
the hope of detecting the mysterious stranger
at the window, he went on his way with a
more elastic step. If he won the pool, could
he not afford to give the one woman in the
world the superb diamonds which he had examined at a jeweller's the week before? He
would be cautious and delay a little, and
await developments.

On the very next evening Ben happened to
run across George Edmunds at the club, and
immediately asked him the question upper-
most in his mind: " Who was the lady
walking home with you from church yesterday ? "

The inquiry was made in the most inno-
cent, off-hand manner, but obviously George
was prepared for it. Be it for the reason

HORACE HAD BEEN ESCORTING THE UNKNOWN IN QUESTION
HOME FROM CHURCH

that he had never forgiven Ben for charging him with being in love before he knew it himself, or for impugning his financial judgment, George had taken sides. He was particularly desirous that Horace Wilson should win the pool, and consequently was on his guard.

He answered, diplomatically, " My wife's mother is staying with us for a few days."

" I congratulate you, George. It wasn't your wife's mother with you yesterday, however. The lady Horace Wilson escorted to your house was no one's mother. Is he attentive to her ? "

" Spying, eh ? " said George. " No, he isn't."

" What's her name ? "

George hesitated. He was on the point of telling ,and then, for no particular reason, thought better of it.

" It will never be Wilson," he replied.

George Edmunds returned to the bosom of his family that night in an anxious frame of mind. He and his wife, the late Virginia Tebbetts, were already at war in regard to the relations between Horace Wilson and their guest, Miss Florence Delaney, and his interview with Ben Davis had made him still more solicitous that his better half should do nothing further to promote the affair.

"It will be the same as robbing Horace of a good thirteen thousand dollars," said he to his spouse. "You should have seen the triumphant, avaricious gleam in Ben's eyes when he told me that he had detected him. Just leave the man alone, Virginia. Provided you let him go his own gait, I feel sure that his natural antipathy to your sex will lead him out of temptation. But if you keep egging him on, the next thing we shall hear is that he is engaged."

"I devoutly hope so, dear. I have made the discovery that Horace Wilson is one of those men whose matrimonial sweetness has been wasted on the desert air of a club long enough. He is peculiarly adapted to be a husband and father, but the girls in the world who would suit him are abnormally scarce. Dear Florence happens to be one of them. He may never meet another; and so the sooner they are engaged the better."

"Then let him find it out for himself. Don't prod him into it."

"No, dear; a bachelor of his age needs to be prodded now and then in order to realize what is best for him. So great is the sexual shyness which a wicked association such as yours engenders, that a woman has to give very clear signs that she is pleased, or the man will run back into his lair again and fancy himself jilted. Don't you remember how I had virtually to offer myself to you before you came to the point?"

"But no third person dragged me up to the halter."

"No; because you see, George, I really liked you almost as much as you did me. But the trouble here is that Florence doesn't know her own mind. It seems there's another."

"Thank goodness."

"Ah, George, don't talk like that. Poor Horace is just crazy about her. He thinks of nothing else. And he needs encouragement so badly. Only this afternoon he said to me, 'I'm afraid it's no use. I'll give it up and go in for the pool. She doesn't care for me more than for the button on one of her boots.' Oh, it was pitiful, George!"

"Who is this another?"

"That's the difficulty. I don't even know definitely that there is another. But I feel morally sure that there is. Otherwise she would accept Horace. It's harassing, for they are just made for each other. I warn you, George, that I am going to do everything that I can to bring them together. I shall invite her frequently to stay, and I shall go where she goes this summer. It was you who were responsible for this hateful Association, and I feel a moral obligation to save Horace Wilson while there is yet time."

"The time to save him, as you call it, will be after he has pocketed the thirteen thousand dollars," said George.

Mrs. Edmunds was a determined woman. Her words were no idle sputterings to be forgotten as soon as spoken. She was resolved to keep the possibility that he might be accepted constantly before the mind of Horace Wilson, and with feminine, feline instinct she reached out for Ben Davis as an ally. She happened to meet him at Tiffany's some fortnight later. He had gone in to have another look at the diamonds, and he was reflecting that the pool would enable him to satisfy admirably his impulse to do the handsome thing by her who was to be his, when he looked up and beheld Mrs. Edmunds watching him. He bit his tongue in vain to keep from blushing. He realized that he had been caught in a very compromising situation. Yet to his relief his observer did not seem to notice it. On the contrary she said: "If you have a spare moment, Mr. Davis, I wish to have a few words with you in regard to our mutual friend, Mr. Wilson. Perhaps you do not know that he is in love."

"I had guessed as much."

"Then you know her?"

"Not well. I have seen her." It would have been more accurate to say that he had seen the tip of her bonnet. But Ben was a diplomat by instinct.

"She is a charming creature. Just the woman for him. He really ought to be married. And all he needs is encouragement— to be egged on. Can I count on you, Mr. Davis, now and then to do a little egging?"

The late Virginia Tebbetts spoke with all the engaging sweetness at her command, and conscious that she had said all that was necessary to enlist him on her side, provided he were willing to yield to the temptation, she glided away and left Ben to his own cogitations.

The result of this interview was twofold. It strengthened Ben's resolution to be cautious and make haste slowly in the matter of committing himself toward his intended, and it gave him an excuse for opening fire on Horace. As Mrs. Edmunds had said, Horace really ought to be married. A word or two of encouragement from him might cement matters and bring about his friend's everlasting happiness. The game was perfectly fair, for Horace knew well enough that the man who was engaged first would lose the pool.

The opportunity came the following week. Ben was returning from Philadelphia, where he had been to call on his Dulcinea, and he ran across Horace in the train. They had the smoking-compartment all to themselves, so Ben opened fire at once.

"I've come to the conclusion, old man," he said, "that there's no happiness like married happiness. I rather expect to be married myself some day." This admission seemed to Ben to be magnanimous, and he proceeded to add, without a qualm, "A little bird has told me that you have only to ask in a certain quarter to be accepted."

"And leave you to gather in the pool?" replied Horace, promptly. "Springes to catch woodcocks, eh?"

"Yes, I should win the pool," said Ben, slowly. "But what is a pool compared with true love? You may lose her, man, if you let mercenary considerations move you."

Horace made no verbal response. He merely sighed — sighed deeply. Ben, who was a diplomat, respected this display of emotion by silence. He bided his time and said, presently, "I understand that she is very charming."

"She is an angel," said Horace. "But I'm not worthy of her, in the first place, and in the second, she doesn't care for me."

"How can you tell until you ask her?" murmured Ben; though, to do him justice, he reminded himself of the murderer of Gonzago, pouring the poison into his victim's ear in the play of one William Shakespeare.

Horace sighed again, more pensively and less hopelessly than before. Just then the

16

train stopped at a way station and Ben took advantage of the five minutes' intermission to telegraph to the florist at Philadelphia :

" Delay lily."

He had given orders that morning to have one sent to her on Easter Sunday, which was the day after to-morrow, but it seemed to him, in view of the entire situation, that he had better suspend active operations until he should ascertain whether Horace's campaign was likely to be long or short. The girl might be one of the kind who would refuse Horace the first time ; in which case there would be a fearful relapse, and months might pass before the sick man could be egged on to a second trial.

The spring slipped away, and so did the summer and autumn, and presently the ground was covered with snow, and Christmas-wreaths were in the windows. On the evening of the twenty-fourth, or Christmas-eve as we call it, the mercury was only five degrees above zero; it was snowing, and those who had put off buying their Christmas presents until the last minute found Jack Frost a too attentive companion. Ben Davis was not among them. He was sitting in his pleasant bachelor's rooms, comfortably established before a glorious fire. He had bought all his Christmas presents, and he had even hung up his own stocking, but he was not thinking of Christmas at the moment. Once or twice he rubbed his hands pleasantly together, as though he were gratified at his own reflections. And indeed they were satisfactory from his point of view. Only the day before yesterday he had had a most interesting interview with his ally and fellow-conspirator, Mrs. George Edmunds, who had complimented him on his egging capabilities, and whose final words had been, "She is coming to stay with us to-morrow, and I shall be egregiously surprised if he doesn't ask her and if she doesn't accept him. It is practically an accomplished fact."

An accomplished fact! With Horace Wilson engaged and out of the way, the pool would be his and he would be free to be as devoted as he pleased to the charmer in Philadelphia. Another Christmas-eve should not find him a lonely bachelor, but a happy Benedict, with the sweetest wife in the world. He had waited the longest, but he had won both the pool and the most charming of her sex. And after all, was he not the one entitled to the pool? But for his prudence and prompt action in the nick of time, there would have been no pool left. It would have gone where the rest of the funds in the "Plimsoll Aëronautic Concern" had gone. Instead, it was invested in a gilt-edged mortgage on improved real estate. Prudence! Caution! These had been the watchwords of his career. They had served him well in business, and now they were to serve him well in love. If only Horace Wilson announced his engagement on Christmas-day, he would offer himself on the first of January, and she should have the diamonds. He rubbed his hands again at the thought, then started, for someone had knocked. It was ten o'clock. Who could be the caller on so cold and stormy a night? "Come in," he cried, and in walked the gentleman of whom he had been thinking, well done up in a heavy coat which was plentifully besprinkled with snow.

"I wish you merry Christmas, Horace. You look like Santa Claus himself."

"I am Santa Claus. By your leave, Ben, I've come for a cigar and a nightcap. Ah!"

he added as he approached the hearth, " I see you have hung your stocking up."

" Yes. I always do that. Some years I wake up and find it empty. But it reminds me of old times to see it there."

" Well, you won't find it empty to-morrow morning. I've come to fill it."

" Brought me a present, eh ? " Ben's pulses bounded joyfully, but his habitual caution bade him speak decorously.

" A good many men would be very glad to find what you will find in your stocking. But very likely you won't care much. Ben, I'm engaged. I dare say you can afford to congratulate me."

Congratulate him ? It was a little awkward to have to jump up and nearly wring a man's hand off when you had just come into a neat $13,500 as the result of his action. Nevertheless, Ben did it with consummate tact and all the semblance of sincerity. Glad ? Of course he was glad ; simply radiant. There was no need to pretend. He shook Horace by the hand again and again, and they both laughed until they nearly cried.

" You have won the pool, old boy, and I

don't care a straw. I'm the luckiest fellow in the world. She's a perfect darling."

"I'm sure she is. I wish you no end of happiness, Horace."

"Do you know her, Ben?"

"No, I caught just a glimpse of her once on George Edmunds's door-steps. Merely the tip of her bonnet. I suspected you, though, from that minute."

"Did you, really? George has been awfully kind; that is, confound him, I mean infernally disagreeable. He did not want me to lose the pool, and so he tried to make out that it would be time enough to think of marrying when the twenty years ran out. But his wife, heaven bless her, and you, Ben, kept my spirits up. If it wasn't one at me it was the other, until finally I took heart and asked her. You were gunning for the pool, of course, Ben. I saw that. But you helped me all the same, and, thanks to you and Virginia Edmunds, I've something to live for now. You don't know, Ben, what an insignificant thing money seems to me to-night. Get married—get married, Ben, as soon as you can."

"Perhaps I may some day," he answered,

significantly, moved by Horace's enthusiasm, for it was no longer necessary to be cautious. "I shall have to drink to bachelorhood alone this year; but between you and me, Horace, I hope for better things some day."

"Don't put it off, Ben. If you only knew —but you don't. I won't bore you. George says I'm as obnoxious to the nerves as a Fourth of July celebration."

"I don't even know her name."

"Florence. Do you remember the day we met on the train coming from Philadelphia? I had just been to see her. Florence Delaney."

Ben looked at him for a moment in silence. "It is a pretty name," he said, quietly.

"And she is an adorable woman."

"Yes."

"I thought you said you didn't know her."

"I was mistaken. I find I do. You are indeed the luckiest man in the world."

Horace glanced at him narrowly, struck by his grave tone and by the quietness of his demeanor. "Poor fellow," he said to himself. "He must be thinking what an infernally dull thing it is to be an old bachelor. I won't remind him of it any longer."

Horace remained until he had finished his cigar. After he had gone Ben sat for a long time with his face in his hands and his head on the table. To think that he had never recognized her on George Edmunds's steps that Sunday morning. He called to mind Horace's speech urging him not to put off being married, and he laughed at his own discomfiture, though there were real tears in his eyes. He said to himself that he was doomed to be an old bachelor to the end of his days. Christmas-eve after Christmas-eve would find him just like this. What a fool he had been. Prudence! Caution! They had served him well, indeed, in the matter of love. He seemed to see them before his mind's sight in mocking letters of fire. He had won the pool ; but what was the pool now? Poor, pitiful schemer that he had been ; he had thrown away the chance of his life.

He walked his room long that night, and when he went to bed it was not to sleep. The sun rose on a city mantled in snow. It was Christmas-day, but Ben felt that he belonged nowhere except at his club. He dined there alone, and after dinner he went into the writing-room and wrote. Merely a few lines ; but when he had finished them he felt better. On the following morning he rose early, for he had a present to buy on his way down town. He was at Tiffany's so promptly that the attendants were still rubbing the aftermath of Merry Christmas from their eyes when he entered. "Let this be delivered as soon as possible. It is a Christmas present I had neglected to buy," he said to the salesman from whom he made his purchase.

An hour and a half later Horace Wilson and his ladylove were sitting on the sofa in Mrs. George Edmunds's drawing-room, when the maid entered with a tolerably large parcel which she delivered to Miss Delaney. Notwithstanding that Miss Delaney was very comfortable where she was, she forsook the sofa in order to examine her belated Christmas present.

"I wonder whom it can be from, Horace," she murmured, feverishly, as young ladies will under such circumstances. But before she undid the parcel she stopped to read the note which accompanied it.

"How very kind of him!" she said, when

she had finished. She looked just a little queer, too. " It's from Mr. Benjamin Davis." And she held out the note.

" Ben Davis? I didn't know you knew him."

" Oh, yes, dear, very well indeed. In fact—" but here Miss Delaney stopped and gave a little laugh, and began busily to undo the parcel.

" In fact what ? " asked Horace.

" Nothing." Then she gave a sudden scream of transport. " Look, Horace, look. Why, they are diamonds — real diamonds. Did you ever see anything so superb ? "

Horace whistled with astonishment. " Diamonds ? I should think they were ! "

But a flush of disquietude presently succeeded the expression of delight on Miss Delaney's face, and she looked up at her lover appealingly. " I really don't see why he sent me such a present. They are lovely, but I don't think I like it."

" You mustn't feel annoyed, dearest," answered Horace, mysteriously. " Ben has tried to do the handsome thing, and he has done it."

" May I really keep them, Horace ? " she asked, almost supplicatingly.

"WHY THEY ARE DIAMONDS—REAL DIAMONDS!"

“Certainly, dear. Ben has sent them on my account, and he has acted very generously. I have a little confession to make, if you will listen. I ought to have told you before, but I haven't had time since yesterday. Ben and I have been members of a club called the Matrimonial Tontine Mutual Benefit Association.” Thereupon Horace told her the whole story—at least he thought he had. “So you see,” he said in conclusion, “Ben, the dear old fellow, has taken it into his head to do the handsome thing. He has practically shared the pool with me.”

“I see,” said Florence Delaney, quietly, but she shook her head with a little sigh and looked queerer than before. Horace, however, did not observe these signs of distrust in his deductions, for he was engaged in reading Ben Davis's letter, which, by the way, was the most commonplace of epistles.

“Dear Miss Delaney,” it ran. “Will you do me the favor to accept these jewels with my sincerest wishes for your future happiness? Wishing you a merry Christmas, I am yours very sincerely, Benjamin Davis.”

It was natural, in view of his understanding of the matter, that the gift of the diamonds should not be concealed by Horace from George Edmunds and his wife. It happened later in the day, when Horace was showing them to Mrs. George, that she remarked, casually, "Now that it is all settled, Horace, I don't mind telling you that I was very much concerned at one time lest Florence would accept Ben Davis."

"What do you mean?" exclaimed our hero, very nearly letting fall the precious stones in his agitation.

"Why, he was the 'another' of whom I was so much afraid, though I didn't let you see I was. I didn't know myself that he was Mr. Davis until a few weeks ago, and when I realized that I had induced him to egg you on to offer yourself to his own sweetheart, I felt like a guilty wretch. But it was too late to draw back then. Why, Horace, how strange you look! I took it for granted that Florence had told you all about it."

"You have merely added just a few paltry details which make me inclined to be sorry that I let Florence keep those diamonds," said Horace, grimly.

"Ah, you won't be so cruel as to take them away now after telling her she could keep them? Besides it would hurt Mr. Davis's feelings. He has really been very generous."

"Confound him, yes. I suppose you are right, though. Poor fellow, how I pity him! I can certainly afford to be a little generous too."

BY HOOK OR CROOK

BY HOOK OR CROOK

BY HOOK OR CROOK

I

TOM NICHOLS owed the beginning of his reputation as an architect to his successful design for the Public Library at Foxburgh. The building was promptly recognized as a tasteful and original conception; consequently new orders came in, not merely for libraries, but for a church or two, several town-halls, a soldiers' monument, a skating-rink, and sundry private residences. In the language of Tom's friends and acquaintance, his affairs were looking up, a pleasant condition which emboldened Mrs. Nichols to have several articles of furniture covered and to buy two new carpets. She explained to Tom that most women would have insisted on having a new house, but that she was attached to the little nest which they had chosen ten years before, when they had married

17

for love in the teeth of the popular refrain,
" What on earth are they going to live on ? "
It was really a very attractive little house,
most conveniently situated, and they might
not be so happy elsewhere.

" Instead of moving, Tom, I intend to entertain more," added Mrs. Nichols. " You
know we have always wished to entertain
freely and never felt able to. Now we can."

Tom nodded approvingly. He did not
wish to move, and he shared his wife's ambition to be hospitable. It was pleasant to
feel that he could afford to invite his friends
to the house without being conscious of the
price of oysters. Their social instincts had
nearly ruined them on several occasions.
Twice at least they had given a little supper
when their exchequer was alarmingly low,
merely because they could not resist the
temptation to take advantage of the witching
hungry hour after the theatre.

" I shall alter very little our way of doing
things, except to do them oftener and to invite a few more people," continued Mrs. Nichols, musingly.

" Exactly my idea, Elizabeth."

" If I did, I should drift straight into the

conventional, every-day, kettle-drum-giving sort of woman, or we should find ourselves in the smart set. Have you ever reflected, Tom, that if you or I had been very rich when we were married, we should have been in the smart set to-day, starved in soul and feeding off gold plates ? What a terrible existence it would be to go on dining with the same little set of people three or four times a week, never meeting any one else, and discussing eternally horses, precious stones, and butlers ! We should never have been willing to ride on bicycles or spend the summer on an abandoned farm. Oh, Tom, however rich we may become, we must never surround ourselves with a gilded wall which shuts out of view all the world and its interest except the limited few who eat truffles in their food every day."

Elizabeth Nichols was rarely outwardly emotional, indeed she passed as a practical, passive woman ; but there was a little quaver of intensity in her closing sentence which prompted Tom to lift his right hand and say, "So help me," by way of expressing his intention not to erect such a wall when he became extremely wealthy.

"We must never lose our independence," she went on, "but I should like to branch out just a little, to have interesting people at the house in an informal way, and entertain occasionally the strangers of note who come to town—literary men, actors—you understand."

Tom nodded again. The proposition was to his liking, for it was evident to him that Mrs. Nichols in branching out did not intend to banish the Welsh rarebit, the oysters in cream, and other delicacies which Tom prided himself on being able to prepare on a blazer so skilfully that the mouths of his friends never ceased to water until the alcohol-lamp went hopelessly out.

"It will be a delightful and improving experience for Minerva also," said Mrs. Nichols. "I feel her on my mind, and if I give her the opportunity to meet agreeable people here, while she is at the receptive age, I shall not blame myself if she throws herself away on some brainless individual hereafter."

Minerva Blair was Mrs. Nichols's first cousin once removed—that is, the only daughter of her first cousin Matilda Blair, who lived a hundred miles away in the country. Minerva was a graduate of Vassar, and a handsome, graceful girl with decided talent as an artist. She had lately come to town to try to make a name for herself with her brush, and had established herself in a studio under the supervision of her cousins Mr. and Mrs. Nichols.

Tom nodded a third time. He admired Minerva Blair. She was natural and unaffected, with abundant spirit and an inquiring mind, and she had style—was in good style, which to his artistic and fastidious eye was all-important. She would draw pleasant young men to his blazer, and at the same time, as Elizabeth had pointed out, she would have the opportunity to cultivate herself by contact with interesting people. Decidedly here was a reason for entertaining if there were no other.

This conversation between Tom and his wife took place in October, and it was the last week in November before all the furniture had been recovered and Mrs. Nichols gave her first entertainment. It was to be a supper party. Eight kindred spirits, including the host and hostess, were to see "Hamlet," and come back to meet the famous actor who impersonated the title rôle at supper. Fancy, therefore, the feelings of Mrs. Nichols when she received a note from her lion at five o'clock on the afternoon of the appointed day stating that he was suffering from the grippe, and that his physician absolutely forbade him to act except on the proviso that he went to bed immediately afterward.

"Tom," called Mrs. Nichols from the top of the stairs, when she heard her husband's step in the hall, "he has the grippe and can't come."

"Who has?" answered Tom, though he knew perfectly well. It was not usual with him to pretend ignorance in order to convict his wife of utter unintelligibility of statement, but he had his reason on this occasion.

His wife, however, disdained to reply. She merely waited for him to come up stairs, then thrust the note at him, exclaiming, "Read for yourself!"

Tom took what seemed to her an everlasting time to complete this operation, as husbands are apt to do when they hold the key to the situation and are trying to be mysterious.

"Well, dear," he said at length, "it might be worse."

“ Worse?   How could it be ? ”

“ If you will allow me to finish, I will tell you.   It might be worse, as I was saying when you interrupted me, for by what now seems to have been a lucky chance, I took it upon myself an hour ago to invite Harold Delaney and Signor Spazzopalli to join us at supper to-night.”

“ Spazzopalli, the new barytone ? ”

“ The very same.”

“ Oh, Tom, that was a stroke of genius.”

“ Harold Delaney, who has him in tow, had been lunching him to-day at the Picnic Club, and was still dilating on his charms when I dropped in there.   Said I to myself, said I, why shouldn’t I ask him to come to-night and have a rarebit with the rest?   Harold jumped at it.   He says he is a soulful creature.”

“ Harold always was a goose, but he seems to have a faculty for intimacies with interesting people.   I really believe, Tom, that the signor is a better card than the other.   He is more of a novelty; scarcely any one has met him.   He is to sing at Mrs. Willoughby Walton’s musical next week at ever-so-much a note, and he *may* sing to us for nothing, if he likes the rarebit. Minerva, you are just in time to hear the news," she added, to her cousin, who came gliding in for a cup of tea.

"Hamlet has the grippe and has given out for to-night, and Tom has invited Spazzopalli instead."

Miss Blair clapped her hands joyously.

"How exciting! His concert yesterday was a grand success, and everyone is dying to meet him personally. Harold Delaney said to me yesterday, as we were leaving the hall, that his voice has all the sentiment of the nightingale without its desperation."

"Harold is coming too," said Mrs. Nichols.

"And not merely Harold," said Tom, with an effort at nonchalance.

"Whom else have you asked?" cried his wife, tragically, divining from his manner that he had a confession to make.

"I have asked Irving K. Baker."

"That man!" Mrs. Nichols sank on the sofa in an attitude of collapse.

"I came bump upon him in the street just after leaving the Picnic Club, and—and Elizabeth, you forget that, if he hadn't been on the committee, my Foxburgh plans might never have been accepted."

"Was that a reason for inviting him to supper to-night? You had all the rest of the year in which to invite him. Oh dear, what shall I do with him?"

"Who is this bone of contention?" asked Minerva.

"A reporter whom we met on the abandoned farm where we stayed summer before last. He fell out of a balloon on the Fourth of July and on to us. Tom couldn't abide him, and would have had a pitched battle with him but for me. He and Professor Strout, his companion in the balloon, both fell in love with the daughter of the abandoned farm, and the Professor won her."

"Oh, I remember. You wrote mother about him. He sounded interesting but a little dreadful."

"He *is* interesting," said Tom, "and he isn't nearly as dreadful as he was. He has improved in appearance, and he tells me he has come here to live. I told him that he must come to see us, at which he seemed to hesitate, and he answered that he was afraid he wasn't much of a hand at meeting society people. That maddened me, for if there is a reportorial trick that I abhor it is that of referring to those who give their daughters in marriage with some degree of ceremony, and when they invite friends to dine don't permit everything edible to be served at once, as 'society people.' 'See here, Baker,' I said, leading him into a convenient doorway so that we might have it out squarely, 'that's stuff. All respectable and intelligent people nowadays are society people. Clergymen's sons and professors' daughters are vying in the effort to be gracious and graceful. The day has passed in this country when to eat in one's shirt sleeves, to lie in one's boots on the sofa, and to go to bed at nine o'clock is significantly indicative of republican virtue, any more than washing one's hands oftener than once a day or wearing a swallow-tail coat in the evening suggests to the sober sentiment of the community a want of moral fibre or a lack of patriotism. When the newspapers sneer at the well-bred as 'society people' they are trying to increase their circulation by consoling the vulgar, and they succeed very imperfectly. It is sheer cant. You are a society person yourself, Baker, and you are proud of it.'"

"Why, Tom, you almost remind me of him

by your tirade. What did he say? " asked Elizabeth.

"That was the strangest part of it. I rather expected he would get angry. Instead, he looked at me in a confused sort of way, and then answered: 'It *is* cant. And what you say is true. It's envy that breeds the sneer on the reportorial pen. As for myself, I've come here to live, and I'd be glad to make acquaintances. Two years ago I needed salting badly, and I'm not entirely cured to-day, but I know a trifle more than I did then. I'll come to see you. How is your lady?' "

"I wish he'd sprinkle a little salt on the word lady in that connection," said Mrs. Nichols.

"It *was* rather blood-curdling, and nearly stifled the generous impulse which the pathos of his surrender and utter humility had aroused in me. I suppose you wish it had. 'Come to-night,' I said. 'My wife has asked a few friends to drop in to supper after the theatre.' And he's coming. You know you always stood up for him, Elizabeth."

"Yes, on an abandoned farm. He was

splendid there. Well, dear, if he's coming, he's coming. Oil and water do not mix, but possibly Signor Spazzopalli and Mr. Irving K. Baker may. It is your party now, Tom, not mine, but I will do all I can for you. There will be plenty to eat, but I warn you that if the affair does not prove an artistic success, I am not to blame."

"I will devote myself to Mr. Baker," said Minerva. "You know I like unconventional people, and I'm sure we shall get on famously together."

Mrs. Nichols's theatre party included, besides themselves and Miss Blair, Mrs. George Swan, Mr. and Mrs. Duncan Seymour, and two single men. Mrs. Swan was a cultivated and attractive woman of refined sensibilities and artistic tastes. She took a keen interest in celebrities, and she had not met Signor Spazzopalli. On the other hand, Mr. and Mrs. Duncan Seymour had met him four times, although he had been in town only three days. On his arrival he had found Mr. Seymour's card with a card of invitation to the Picnic Club. By the next morning's post he had received a note running, "My dear Signor Spazzopalli, will

you come to us for luncheon to-day at two?
Yours cordially, Louise Seymour." The
same afternoon, after luncheon, Mrs. Seymour had taken him to drive in a phaeton
for an hour and a half, and she considered
him now one of her oldest friends, and spoke
of him as "that dear signor." She was a
fine figure of a woman, with a perfervid
manner. She produced the effect of wishing
to embrace one on the spot, which kept people who believed her glowing complexion to
be artificial in constant terror. She had
taken a strong fancy to Minerva Blair, and
declared the intention of making her a bohe-
mian. She deemed herself one, and she was
fond of saying that she did not see why men
should have all the fun. By way of living
up to her principles she smoked occasional
cigarettes, took a small gin cocktail before
dinner when her husband took his, and used
minor oaths. Mr. Seymour was a hard-
working and somewhat talented musician,
who sympathized with his wife's ambition
to tame lions, and approved of her desire to
be a good comrade. One of the single men
was a rather weather-beaten beau who spoke
languages and was considered available where

foreigners were concerned.   The other was a playwright of growing repute.

Signor Spazzopalli and Harold Delaney arrived a few minutes after the theatre party. Harold was what might be called a social pilot-fish to celebrities. He could rush in where women would hesitate, and consequently could beard a lion in his den, or bath if need be, and put a leading-string about him.   He and Mrs. Seymour were pals, as that lady called it, and he invariably descanted on the attractions of the musician and his wife to the animals he had in tow.

Mrs. Seymour straightway took possession of the singer, and proceeded to exploit the rest of the company for his comprehension. She beckoned to Minerva to come and be introduced.

"Signor, this is a friend of mine who adores your voice—Miss Minerva Blair, a Vassar girl and an artist. She is a college graduate, you know, and you must see her pictures."

Spazzopalli bent his long, lean figure in a profound bow. He saw before him a very pretty girl, and beauty in any form appealed to him.

AFTER THE THEATRE PARTY

"I think I never enjoyed anything so much as that last song of yours yesterday," she said, with simple directness. "It must be glorious to be able to enthrall people so that they seem to touch the stars for a little while at least."

"Mademoiselle is too kind. Yes, I enjoy my art. And it pleasures me to hear I make people feel as you say."

He spoke without hesitation, in spite of the quaintness of his diction. Eager enthusiasm shone, too, from his large dark eyes. They were the most striking feature of his countenance, which otherwise was conventional with its smoothly parted hair and closely trimmed pointed brown beard.

"Isn't he devilish handsome?" whispered Mrs. Seymour in a fairly audible tone, as Mrs. Swan claimed the singer's attention by a dulcet remark.

The necessity for answering this inquiry was obviated for Minerva by the entrance of Irving K. Baker, whose aspect of novelty plainly altered the current of Mrs. Seymour's thoughts. "Why, who is that?" she asked.

"Mr. Irving K. Baker, a friend of the

Nicholses," answered Minerva. "He is connected with the press, I believe."

"How interesting!" said Mrs. Seymour, rhapsodically. "I do like new people. I wonder what he does?"

Mr. Baker's toilet was a relief to Elizabeth, though she had been prepared to receive him cordially in a cardigan jacket, in case he should appear in that form of evening dress. She was an eminently considerate and reasonable woman in such matters. For instance, though she greatly preferred, for æsthetic reasons, to have her maids wear caps, she invariably yielded to their scruples that it was a badge of service, and merely insisted that they should do their hair neatly. But she liked to see conventions respected, if no one's feelings were lacerated or principles violated thereby, and it was with a glow of satisfaction that she perceived Mr. Baker had on a swallow-tail coat, and that no one could cavil at his outward appearance. This agreeable consciousness imparted perhaps extra cordiality to her greeting.

"It is very pleasant to see you again," she said, beaming upon him. "And what do you hear of our mutual friends the Strouts?"

"In the last letter which the professor wrote me he stated that he had decided to turn his talents as a juggler to account. Henceforward from May to November he will devote himself to navigating the air, and from November to May he will practise necromancy, disguised as Herr Falkenburg, late wizard extraordinary to the King of Greece."

"To the King of Greece?"

"A mere figment of the fancy, a pardonable advertising dodge which will add a certain glamour to his impersonations and yet injure in no respect those whom it deceives."

"And Maretta? What does she think of this?" inquired Mrs. Nichols.

"She is his trump card. She figures nightly as Almeda, the Georgian beauty and gypsy mind-reader. The Georgian women are the most beautiful in the world, and Professor Strout states that none but the initiated for a moment suspect that the freeborn daughter of an abandoned farm is not a genuine flower of Asian soil. They are billed to perform here in a fortnight."

"Next week? Tom, do you hear that? We must all go to see them. Fancy Maretta as an Asian mind-reader! I wonder if she still says 'Oh my!'"

Mr. Baker colored a little. "Our women have great powers of adaptability," he said. "We should probably find her wonderfully changed."

"But no less charming, I'm sure," said Elizabeth, who felt a little ashamed of herself.

Supper was now ready, or rather the company seated themselves at table, while Tom toyed with one blazer and Duncan Seymour, by special appointment, with another. There was to be a choice between Welsh rarebit à la Nichols and oysters in cream à la Seymour, and each of the cooks in question looked gravely important in his struggles with the raw materials. Minerva Blair found herself next to Signor Spazzopalli and opposite Mr. Baker. She remembered her promise to devote herself to the reporter, but she found some difficulty in doing so, owing to the fact that Signor Spazzopalli, after a preliminary show of deference to his hostess, had turned his head in her direction, and was giving utterance to a flow of words the charm of which was heightened for her by

the quaint turn of his sentences and by the
accent with which they were spoken. She
saw, as in a dream, cheese and beer galore
dissolve into a turbid sea and stiffen into a
quagmire. She heard without hearing the
conversation around her, and the food which
she put to her lips—was it oysters à la Seymour or rarebit à la Nichols? She could not
have stated. And the dear signor? Alike
the blandishments of Mrs. Swan and the
minor oaths of Mrs. Duncan Seymour, the
pleasant prattle of one of the single men and
the genial stories of Mr. Baker, seemed lost
upon him. He was devotion itself to Minerva Blair, and after the blazers had given
up their feast and grown cold, he seated
himself at the piano and sang " Non è ver "
in a tremendous manner. Here was a ten-
strike for Mrs. Nichols. She forgave him
all. He had done unbidden what she had
fervently longed for, and feared that he
might not do. No matter what the cause of
his singing, he had sung; and what is more,
he was going to sing again.

" Wasn't it damnably fine ? " whispered
Mrs. Seymour, squeezing Elizabeth's hand.
It was because Mrs. Seymour's oaths were

apt to be utterly inappropriate that other women did not take offence at them. Mrs. Nichols, who naturally was elated, even squeezed her hand in return.

Spazzopalli sang this time Tosti's " Good-by," and there was no mistaking his meaning. He was singing at and for Minerva in true Italian style, and yet, of course, not so demonstratively as to make his homage otherwise than complimentary to her. She was still in a dream. Her eyes were not lowered ; she simply looked transported and unusually handsome. Mr. Baker could scarcely take his gaze off her. But she had forgotten Mr. Baker's existence.

Mrs. Seymour glided up to her at the end of the second song and nearly embraced her. " You have bowled him over, dear. He sees no one else in the room. You naughty, lucky girl. Now I'm going to plan a nice little luncheon for you this week. There is a ladies' room, you know, at the Picnic Club, and I'll get Duncan to make arrangements for a party of four. You and the signor, and Baker and I. Duncan has engagements and couldn't come. Baker's queer, but he's interesting. We'll have a stunning old time.

Now don't invent any excuses," she added, in repulse of Minerva's look of shy protestation. " Let yourself go, child. Life is dregs unless you let yourself go now and then."

Fifteen minutes later the party had withdrawn, except Irving K. Baker, who, at his host's instigation, had remained to light a cigar. The newspaper man—he was now on the editorial staff of the largest paper in the city—had a certain fascination for Tom. He was curious in regard to him and interested in his development. There was nothing hackneyed about him, even though he was capable of flying in the face of traditional sensibilities. Tom was conscious of running the risk of becoming irritated, but he could not resist the temptation of dallying with him.

Baker started to go as soon as his cigar was lighted, but after putting on his overshoes and a muffler, he paused and said, " What was the name of the profane lady ? "

Tom was nonplussed for a moment, then answered, with a laugh, " Oh, you mean Mrs. Duncan Seymour. Her bark is worse than her bite, Baker. I mean her swear words are all on the surface."

"She has honored me with an invitation to luncheon."

"You should accept by all means. She's an enterprising, kind-hearted woman, whose chief fault is that she likes to pose. She believes that little vulgar eccentricities give her artistic standing, but she means nothing wrong by them. I assure you that Mrs. Seymour is very kind."

Tom was conscious somehow of being on the defensive, and of feeling the necessity of championing his guests so far as he could justly do so in the presence of this former critic of " society people."

"And Miss Blair, who is she?"

"She's a cousin of my wife, a college graduate and an art student, who has come here recently to live. I'm sure you'd like her."

"I like her already. She's an exceptionally charming woman."

Tom's satisfaction at being able to praise this second subject of conversation without stint received a slight check from Mr. Baker's impressive tone. It made him think of the evening when the reporter had announced to him his intention to make the present Mrs.

Alvin Strout his wife within six hours after he had been introduced to her.

"All young girls are very much alike, however," Tom added, with some duplicity.

"On the contrary, I see great differences in them, far greater differences than between rose and rose, for instance," said Mr. Baker, nodding at a vase of flowers which stood on the hall table. "She is a very beautiful young lady," he continued. "It will be a pity if that signor carries her off."

"What!" asked Tom, overwhelmed by the unconventional frankness of this remark.

"Signor Spazzopalli. He has his eye on her."

"They never met until this evening, my dear sir."

"It is a case of love at first sight, then. These foreigners come over here to take our money, and they sneer at us behind our backs. They have no interest in the institutions of this country; they regard it simply as a mint where they can fill their pockets and go home again without a thought as to our aspirations. Miss Minerva Blair should marry an American."

"Amen to that with all my heart," said

Tom. " But, frankly, I do not see any immediate prospect of her marrying anybody.

" I trust that you are correct in your supposition. Perhaps," added Mr. Baker, reflectively, as he stood on the door-step, " my remarks may savor to you of impertinence and I seem to meddle. My interest in the young lady in question must be my excuse. I have only to state that if at any time affairs reach a crisis, I beg that you will not hesitate to call upon me. I may be able to assist you in this connection. Good-night."

II

One evening about a fortnight later Mrs. Nichols was sitting at her fireside absorbed in contemplation. Tom was dining with a club of his fellow-architects, so that she had only her own thoughts for company. These thoughts were far from gratifying. She was revolving the problem which, according to Mrs. Duncan Seymour, who had visited her that afternoon, was agitating society—what was to be the upshot of Signor Spazzopalli's intense devotion to her cousin, Minerva

Blair? Mrs. Seymour had called in order to assure her that the rumor that the signor had a wife in Italy had been carefully investigated by Harold Delaney, and shown to be utterly without foundation. "I should be glad to know he had six wives, if we could only prove it," Mrs. Nichols murmured to herself as she recalled the speech. It annoyed her to think that everyone should take for granted she desired the match, when she really abominated the idea of one. Minerva Blair marry a foreigner! Minerva Blair, whose development had been a source of intense interest to her ever since the day she had learned of her young cousin's intention to enter college! She had watched her and been proud of her, and she had encouraged her to devote herself to art as a profession, when Minerva's own father and mother would have had her return home and become a conventional country daughter of the house. And now she was to be whisked off by an ardent Italian and merge her individuality in the unknown possessor of a splendid voice! It seemed to Mrs. Nichols almost as though she were about to lose a second self; for she was fond of saying to

Tom that Minerva was what she might have been had she gone to college, given her artistic capabilities a chance, and refused to sacrifice her aspirations to the pertinacious advances of a struggling young architect. But—and Mrs. Nichols frowned despairingly at the reflection—suppose Minerva were really in love with Spazzopalli, anyone who interfered might be blighting the girl's happiness for life. There was the rub, and Mrs. Nichols tapped her foot by way of expressing her perplexity.

At that moment Mr. Irving K. Baker entered, and, as Elizabeth rose to greet him, his request to her husband to apply to him, if at any time he could be of service in this connection, came into her mind. She and Tom had enjoyed several hearty laughs over it, but now somehow the idea of appealing to him did not seem to her in her present frame of mind quite so preposterous. Perhaps he would be able to think of some point of attack which had escaped her; very possibly he might know something fatal against Signor Spazzopalli—that he really was married, for instance, Harold Delaney to the contrary notwithstanding, or that he was a vicious character. Newspaper men know many things which are hidden from the world at large, and this might be one of them. Tom had told her that evening before he went to his dinner-party that he had not been able to glean a single disreputable item against him. What a triumph it would be to be able to confront him on his return with splendid damning evidence!

These reflections passed through Mrs. Nichols's mind as she listened to her visitor's opening remarks, which included an announcement that Professor and Mrs. Alvin Strout had arrived in town, and that he counted on the pleasure of taking Mrs. Nichols and her husband and Mr. and Mrs. Duncan Seymour and Miss Minerva Blair to one of their performances. Mrs. Nichols further reflected that Mr. Baker, in spite of his lack of social experience, evidently possessed social instincts, in that he was trying to kill three birds with a single stone—one bird being Tom and herself, who had invited him to supper, another bird being the Seymours, who had invited him to luncheon and been generally kind to him, and the third bird being Minerva, whom he evidently desired to kill for her own sweet self. She answered that so far as she could speak for the others she had every reason to think they would all be charmed to go. As she did so the conundrum propounded itself to her, as conundrums of this kind sometimes will, in case she were forced to choose between Spazzopalli and Irving K. Baker for Minerva, which of the two she would select. In her anxiety to decide she found herself examining the young man attentively. He looks honest, she thought, and as though he has ideas of his own, however odd they may be ; he has spruced himself since the day he fell from the balloon, and appears very much like everybody else. This diagnosis did not enable her to decide whether she would adjudge him less undesirable than the signor as a husband for Minerva, but she said to herself : "I will consult him as to what we can do. He will never realize how queer it is of me."

"Mr. Baker," she said, a few moments later, seizing a favorable opportunity, "do you happen to know anything definite concerning Signor Spazzopalli—more than we who met him in society see and know ? I have a par-

ticular reason for wishing to be told everything there is to tell, so I take the liberty of
asking you the question."

Mr. Baker shook his head. "What is it
you wish to find out?" he added, rather eagerly. "Perhaps as a newspaper man I might
be able to assist you."

"You do not happen to know, for instance, whether he is married or not?"

"Married? Have you heard that he is
married? It would be the simplest thing in
the world to ascertain by cabling. I will
cable to-morrow, at my expense, and find out
for you, Mrs. Nichols." He stopped short
and looked at her inquiringly as though a
new idea had struck him. "Would you like
to discover that he is married?"

Mrs. Nichols hesitated a moment, then,
with the engaging frankness of one who, having seized a bull by the horns, appreciates
that she must adapt herself to the situation,
answered: "I am going to take you into my
confidence, Mr. Baker. Signor Spazzopalli
is paying what appears to be serious attention to my cousin, Miss Blair. We have reason to believe that he may wish to marry her.
One solution of the matter, of course, would

be to ascertain that he is already married to someone else ; but inquiries made by others lead me to believe that there is little hope of that."

"But you would be glad to find it true? You are opposed to the match?"

"I am opposed to nothing that would lead to my cousin's happiness. But I will admit that I do not fancy the idea of her marriage to this foreigner."

"If you will allow me to make the observation, Mrs. Nichols, I have, on every occasion where an opportunity for the display of wisdom has presented itself, had reason to admire your sagacity and good sense."

"Thank you," said Elizabeth, with a little courtesy. "And it is because you have such a fresh, original way of looking at things that I have dared to ask your advice. Now we are quits. But let me say right here, Mr. Baker, that if I believed in my heart that my cousin were really in love with this man, I would rather lose my tongue than breathe a word of conspiracy against him. I have not talked with her on the subject, for she has not broached it to me, and that has sealed my lips. I am sure, though, that she is fas-

"I AM GOING TO TAKE YOU INTO MY CONFIDENCE"

cinated by him, and under the spell of the
glamour which his magnificent voice casts
about him. She is young, ardent, and im-
pressionable, and I firmly believe that his influence is merely a spell, which any—er—
prosaic facts concerning him would dissipate.
I wish at least to discover all that I can concerning him, so that she may make her choice
with her eyes open. It may be bias and prej-
udice which affects me, but I cannot help
feeling that he is not altogether worthy of
her, Mr. Baker."

"Amen, madam, amen! He is no more
worthy of her than the swine is worthy of
the pearl which tradition casts into the sty
to typify human squandering."

"And yet, really, Mr. Baker, there is nothing definite against him."

"We must discover something." Baker
pressed his thin, nervous lips together and
felt of his forehead. At length he tapped it.
"I think I appreciate the situation," he said.
"As I understand it, there has been as yet no
offer of marriage?"

"None to my knowledge. Minerva would
surely have told me."

"And you would be pleased to have

something happen before matters reach a crisis?"

"Happen?" echoed Elizabeth, in a tone of some solicitude, induced by the thought of the sudden disappearance of the signor over a bridge or down a well.

Mr. Baker was quick to divine her suspicions. "I mean," he said, with a sweep of his hand, by which he intended to relegate to the winds such base imaginings, "that you would be pleased to have this foreigner by his own agency show himself in his true colors, so that the glamour which now blinds Miss Minerva Blair's eyes may be swept away forever."

"That would be very nice," said Mrs. Nichols, propitiatingly.

"I say 'by his own agency,'" continued Mr. Baker, gravely, "for I have taken it for granted that in a transaction of this kind mere newspaper enterprise would be distasteful to you. Of course it would be a simple matter, and the idea at first struck me as propitious, to manufacture a wife and children for Signor Spazzopalli by special cablegram from Rome. But apart from the duplicity of such a proceeding, which, knowing as I do the views held by you and Mr. Nichols on the proper limits of reportorial activity, I am sure you would refuse to countenance, there is the further consideration, to which you have already referred, of Miss Blair's happiness. In spite of the adage, ' All is fair in love and war,' I should scorn to lower the reputation of this foreigner in her regard by false or dishonest evidence. He must contribute to his own ruin."

"I am very much relieved to hear you say so, Mr. Baker. Indeed, it would be utterly impossible for me to allow you to proceed on any other understanding. My desire is to discover any shortcomings which Signor Spazzopalli may have, not to injure him by fabrication. My cousin evidently believes him to be wholly sincere, true, and irreproachable, and my conviction is that she will marry him, unless—unless she changes her mind." Elizabeth gave a nervous laugh. "There is the situation, and I must confess that it does not look very promising. Does it ? "

"I consider it far from hopeless. At any rate, Mrs. Nichols, you may feel sure that I will devote myself body and soul to the undertaking. You shall hear from me very soon."

" You are not going already ? "

" Yes. There is not a moment to be lost. We newspaper men know the importance of keeping our fingers on the forelock of time. Have you a telephone ? "

" Yes."

" Matters may reach a point where a witness—a witness whose testimony would be entirely convincing to Miss Blair—would be indispensable. In such an emergency am I authorized to ring you up ? "

" I suppose so," said Elizabeth, a little disconcerted. The detective-like determination of her visitor was almost appalling.

" Good-night," he said, holding out his hand.

" You have a plan already, I see."

" I have an idea, but it may end in smoke. Good-night, Mrs. Nichols."

When he had gone, Elizabeth knew scarcely whether to laugh or to cry. Into what sort of a compact had she entered, and where would it lead her? To be sure, her fellow-conspirator had pledged himself to do nothing which would lead her to the gallows or injure her self-respect, but what did she really know about him? What horrible breach of taste might he not commit which would drag her into unpleasant notoriety and wound the sensibilities of her cousin? There was a possibility of that, indeed; at least she could not claim a sufficient knowledge of Mr. Baker's mental processes and habits to be absolutely sure that he would be discreet. And yet she had entered into the conspiracy with her eyes open, because she was impressed with the idea that if anyone could help her in this quandary he could, and because she believed he could be trusted. As she had told him to his face, his thoughts had freshness and originality; he was not tied down by codes and filigree considerations. Some mode of relief might enter his head which would never enter hers.

"Tom, Tom," she said to her husband when he came home an hour later, "you may see my picture in the *Police Gazette* before I am a month older."

Tom Nichols did not take so serious a view of the situation as this. The idea that his wife had unbosomed herself to Mr. Baker amused him chiefly. He summed up his opinion of the case by saying : " After his assurances, I think that you can feel moderately safe that he will do nothing compromising. What I wonder at is your confidence in his ability to find out anything about our musical friend. A bogus cablegram might be in his line, but I doubt his capacity."

"You have always done Mr. Baker injustice, Tom, merely because he is different from you and me. It is just because he *is* different that I have such faith in him. After the first glow of reportorial activity he saw the impossibility of the cablegram as fully as I did."

For the next few days Elizabeth was on tenter-hooks, but no message came from Mr. Baker. She kept her ear constantly on the alert for the telephone-bell, and answered every call in person, only to listen to the butcher or the grocer. On the fourth day came a note signed by him which brought her heart into her mouth, but it was only to tell her that he had secured tickets to see the Strouts for the following week. Not a word on the other matter to which he had vowed to devote himself body and soul. Elizabeth said " Pshaw!" and threw his note into the fire.

On the tenth day Mrs. Duncan Seymour, whose husband was absent from town for a few days, dined with them. It was a lowering, oppressive night out-doors, and the weather bureau had issued prophecies of an electrical storm as a sort of midwinter travesty on summer.

"I have a new devoted admirer," said Mrs. Seymour in the midst of dinner. "You would never guess—Baker. He says he has been bitten by the tarantula of society, and apparently I am the tarantula personified. He utterly disapproves of me, but can't resist my fascination. Now as for you, my dear," she added, "he admires you unreservedly."

"Elizabeth has bound herself hand and foot—" began Tom, but his wife interjected a commanding "'sh!" which he felt constrained to obey.

"This sounds interesting," said Mrs. Seymour, with an appealing glance at Mr. Nichols.

"I positively forbid you to go on, Tom," said Elizabeth.

Mrs. Seymour looked from one to the other. "There is a mystery here," she said. "*He* will tell me; I will hypnotize him if he refuses. What do you think, Elizabeth? I have bet him a pair of gloves that Signor Spazzopalli marries Minerva. He declares it will never be. He is almost violent on the subject. One would almost suppose that he knew something definite, so positive is he."

Mr. Nichols gave a low chuckle.

"Behave yourself, Tom," said his wife. "Louise," she added, "I wish to change the conversation."

There were no further allusions to Mr. Baker after dinner, and at ten o'clock Mrs. Seymour's carriage was announced. Just then there was a distant but distinct rumble heralding the approach of the storm.

"Old Prob is right for once," said Tom. "You will just have time, Mrs. Seymour, to get home before the thunder and lightning set in."

At that instant the telephone-bell rang energetically.

"Mercy!" cried Elizabeth. "Who can be calling us up at this hour?"

"Perhaps the storm is making the electrical fluid rampant," suggested Mrs. Seymour.

"Or it may be Mr. Baker," said Tom, facetiously.

Ting-a-ling — a-ling — a-ling began the telephone-bell again.

At the mention of the word " Baker," Elizabeth darted from the room and dashed downstairs to the instrument.

" Holloa ! "

" Is that Mrs. Nichols ? "

" Yes. "

" I'm Mr. Baker. It's very important that you come at once to Leblanc's restaurant. I invite you and Mr. Nichols to supper, and I have every reason to believe that before an hour elapses we shall have won."

" To-night ! It is going to thunder and lighten."

" We have been providentially aided by the elements. It is to-night or probably never."

Women think rapidly when they think at all. Mrs. Nichols remembered that Mrs. Seymour's carriage was at the door, and a sudden impulse seized her. Would it not add sweetness to the possibly impending triumph of Mr. Baker to win his pair of gloves in the presence of her guest?

" Mrs. Duncan Seymour is dining with us? May I bring her too ? "

" By all means."

“We’ll come at once then.”

“Tom,” she said, turning to her husband and Mrs. Seymour, who had been lured by curiosity half-way down the back stairs, “we’re to take supper to-night at Leblanc’s restaurant with Mr. Baker. You too, Louise. He has just invited us.”

“Now this is what I call damnably exciting—exciting and shrouded in mystery,” said Mrs. Seymour.

“To-night! Are you crazy, my dear?” asked her husband. “Drag us out in this storm?”

“I am going, Tom,” said Elizabeth, firmly.

“And I am going, Mr. Nichols,” said Mrs. Seymour.

“Then there is no help for me but to go too,” said he.

Within five minutes they were in Mrs. Seymour’s carriage on the way to Leblanc’s, which was only a short distance from the house. It had not begun to rain, but the sky was lurid with the approaching storm and the thunder was getting vehement. Mrs. Seymour sought explanation by a question or two, but Elizabeth sat tongue-tied. As their vehicle stopped at the entrance Mr.

Baker opened the carriage-door, and with merely a word of greeting led the way past the public restaurant upstairs into a private room. The table was laid for four.

"We have been providentially aided by the elements," he repeated in a whisper to Elizabeth as he helped her to remove her wraps. "Does she know?"

"Nothing. Are you going to win the gloves?"

"I believe so. He is there," he added, nodding at the wall.

"Spazzopalli? In the next room?"

"Yes."

What could it mean? Elizabeth felt excited but dazed. Mrs. Seymour glanced around her with a curious smile. As for Tom, he promptly obeyed Mr. Baker's invitation to sit down and partake of the tempting viands which were set before them.

"You will pardon me," said their host, "if I am unable to give you my individual attention. You will know why presently."

"We can't imagine what this is all about," said Tom. "Can we, Mrs. Seymour? But these oysters look very good, even if I did not cook them."

Mr. Baker had vanished into what seemed to be a closet in the side of the room adjoining that in which he had declared Signor Spazzopalli to be. He popped out his head several times by way of keeping the eye of courtesy on his guests, and disappeared promptly again after a few solicitous inquiries. Tom was the only one of the trio who was able to eat. Mrs. Nichols's appetite was ruined by excited anticipation, Mrs. Seymour's by burning curiosity. The thunder-storm had broken, and it was audibly raining torrents, while every few moments the lightning, closely followed by a crashing peal, was so unusual as to attract even their absorbed attention.

Mr. Baker peeped from the door again. "Mrs. Nichols," he said, "will you come this way? Only Mrs. Nichols," he was obliged to add, for Mrs. Seymour rose also, and Tom looked inquisitive.

With a tripping heart Elizabeth obeyed orders. She found herself in a small compartment lighted by a single jet. It was evidently designed to serve as a pantry to either or both rooms, for there was a dumb-waiter in one end and a counter along the

MR. BAKER HAD VANISHED

wall. In the middle of the wall over the counter was an aperture guarded by a slide. The slide was now only partially drawn so as to afford a glimpse of the other room. On the counter was a large black box which Mr. Baker pushed to one side as she entered. "Look through the hole," he whispered.

To do so Elizabeth was obliged to stoop. What she saw was a man and a woman seated at a table at supper. The man was Signor Spazzopalli. He was bending devotedly toward the woman with the air of one bent upon ingratiating himself. The woman was extremely pretty and piquant, suggesting by both her air and costume an actress. Somehow it seemed to Elizabeth that she had seen her before.

"Do you recognize her?" whispered Mr. Baker.

A sudden intuition seized Elizabeth. "Maretta!" she gasped.

Mr. Baker nodded delightedly. He deftly closed the slide to render conversation less hazardous, though, as subsequently appeared, the waiter who was serving the supper had received instructions to approach the slide now and then when in the room in order to give the impression that it was in actual use.

"He is desperately enamoured of her."

"And she with him?"

"Not a bit of it. The idea came to me when I was at your house the other evening, and I went straight to her hotel the next morning, where I found her alone. 'Maretta,' said I, 'I loved you sincerely, and tried to make you Mrs. Irving K. Baker. The professor cut me out. I have come in the name of auld lang-syne to ask you a great favor. A young friend of mine, a beautiful young lady, is in the thrall of a spaghetti-eating Italian, and I need your aid.' 'Tell me all about it,' she said, and I did. She got her husband's permission, and here she is."

"I do not quite understand," said Elizabeth.

"She wrote to him and led him to believe that she was fascinated by his manly form and mellifluous voice. He nibbled at the bait, and here we have him. Don't give yourself any concern on the score of propriety, Mrs. Nichols," he added, noting a cloudy look on Elizabeth's brow, "Maretta is spotless as an angel. She accepted his invitation to supper only after consultation with me. He means mischief, though."

"And what are you going to do now that you have them here?"

Mr. Baker tapped his black box significantly.

"You will see in a minute. You invite your husband and Mrs. Seymour to witness the finale, if you like," he said, opening the slide cautiously to its full capacity.

Just then there came a glare of lightning fiercer than its fellows, and a crash of thunder which shook the building.

"Oh my!" exclaimed Maretta, in genuine dismay.

"It is she, sure enough," murmured Elizabeth. "How handsome she has grown to be! Really, Mr. Baker, you must tell me what you mean by all this."

"Tell the others while I get ready. This storm shows that Providence is in league with us."

Elizabeth stepped into the room and beckoned to the others.

"You have been infernally cruel," said Mrs. Seymour. "I am critically ill with suppressed curiosity."

When they entered the closet Mr. Baker had filled up more than half the aperture with the black box, into which he was peering after the manner of a photographer. There was still a vacant hole, however, through which Tom and Mrs. Seymour looked.

"The villain!" whispered Mrs. Seymour. "I have seen him gaze into Minerva's face like that a dozen times. This is confoundedly perfidious. Who is she?"

"Yes, who is she?" asked Tom. "I admire the brute's taste, anyway."

"'Sh! Can't you tell? It is Almeda, the Georgian beauty, *alias* Maretta Strout."

Tom gave a low whistle.

"Mrs. Nichols," said Mr. Baker, rising from the squatting posture in which he had been peering into his box, "please take your husband's place, and when you and Mrs. Seymour see anything particularly edifying, say 'Now.' If you, Mr. Nichols, will hold this pan of combustibles, and when your wife gives the word, touch it off with this taper, I'll attend to the rest. To do the trick successfully we must all act together. That's right," he added, as another flash of lightning interrupted him ; "the more of that the better for us."

Mrs. Nichols took her place in silence beside Mrs. Seymour. It was obvious now to her what was going to happen.

Spazzopalli and Maretta had finished eating, and he was talking to her with an intenser manner, now and again raising his glass of champagne and pledging her ardently. She sat demure, with a playful smile on her lips ; only once she shot a glance toward the ambush, as though to ask how much longer the comedy was to last.

"The monster!" murmured Mrs. Seymour. "He must catch one of those fiery love-sick glances. He looked just like that when he sang 'Non è ver' to Minerva."

Mrs. Nichols sat very still. Though she was half conscious that she disapproved of the whole proceeding, there was a deep fascination in the duty which had been imposed upon her, and an inclination to carry it out as completely as possible. She watched the couple with lynx-like scrutiny, intent to note every change of Spazzopalli's expression. If her cousin was to be avenged or disillusionized in this strange manner, the blow must

be struck deftly and artistically. Thrice
Mrs. Seymour nudged her as some fresh
glance or gesture was manifested, but she
did not yet feel satisfied. Meantime the
fury of the storm waxed, and ever and again
vivid flashes of lightning, of which at least
one of the pair at the supper-table seemed
wholly regardless, came in from the night.

Suddenly, as though the demure smiling
calm of the woman had maddened him,
Spazzopalli leaned forward across the nar-
row table and caught Maretta's hands in his.
For an instant she struggled, then either ap-
preciating the advantages of the situation, or
realizing that the firm grasp of his long fingers was not to be frustrated, she remained
passive, and smiled back at him languorous-
ly. Lured by his success and her demeanor,
he leaned forward to bring his lips close to
hers. Just as they seemed to touch, and
with Mrs. Seymour's " He is going to kiss
her! " still in her ears, Elizabeth, in a tense
voice, said " Now! " and quick as thought
there was a vivid flare of light, which suggested for a moment to those inside the
closet that Vesuvius was let loose, and
caused Spazzopalli to leap to his feet in the

HE WAS TALKING TO HER WITH AN INTENSER MANNER

belief that the house had been struck by lightning. The smoke which followed the glare by which the flash-light photograph was obtained concealed everything for a moment from Elizabeth, but she heard distinctly Maretta's "Oh my!" which even foreknowledge of what was to happen and the consciousness of her Georgian nationality could not repress. When she could see, Spazzopalli had opened the door and was calling, loudly: "Garçon! garçon! The lightning is in the house!"

Before the summons was answered, Mr. Baker had noiselessly closed the slide and opened the closet door.

"If you will step into the room," he said, "I shall be able in a few minutes to tell you if the flash-light photograph is a success."

Tom and his wife and Mrs. Seymour obeyed orders, and Mr. Baker shut himself up again in the closet to make the necessary investigation.

"Well, of all extraordinary performances, that is the masterpiece," burst out Tom. "I don't quite know whether to throttle Baker as a sneak, or to applaud him as a genius."

"I think it was very clever of him," said

20

Mrs. Seymour, promptly. "The signor deserved to be shown up if ever man did. The false, hypocritical villain! When I think of Minerva I feel like crying. Mr. Baker did nothing, Mr. Nichols, but put temptation in his way, and if a man who pretends to be in love with one woman throws her over for another, why shouldn't he be photographed and branded as a faithless wretch? Don't you think so, Elizabeth?"

Mrs. Nichols had seated herself at the dismantled supper-table, and, buried in pensive thought, was spearing the same oyster over and over again. She did not answer, and before Mrs. Seymour had time to repeat her question, Mr. Baker reappeared with a radiant countenance.

"It is perfect!" he cried. "You caught him, Mrs. Nichols, at exactly the right moment. I congratulate you heartily; and, Mrs. Seymour, you owe me a pair of gloves."

"What makes you think she does?" asked Elizabeth, coldly, making another thrust at the mangled oyster.

"Because when Miss Blair confronts Signor Spazzopalli with this photograph, I assure you that he will renounce any matrimonial expectations which he now entertains," said the reporter, blithely.

"And who is to confront Miss Blair with it?"

"You, of course, Elizabeth," said Mrs. Seymour at once.

"I took it for granted that you would do that, Mrs. Nichols," said Mr. Baker, in a tone of surprise. "But if you think I ought to——"

"If anyone does it, it will be I," said Elizabeth, interrupting him almost fiercely. "I must ask you, Mr. Baker, as a particular favor, never to breathe a word to her on the subject—to her or to anyone else."

"I shall obey your directions implicitly," said Mr. Baker, with a sweeping bow. "I have tried to please you, Mrs. Nichols, and to live up to the spirit of our compact. If I have failed to satisfy you I am very sorry."

Elizabeth blushed deeply. It was at the word "compact." But the pathetic solicitude of his tone awakened her sense of justice. She put out her hand and said, "Goodnight, Mr. Baker; you have been extremely kind and — and ingenious, and if matters have taken a somewhat different turn than I expected, it is only I who am to blame. Good-night."

Mr. Baker looked a little nonplussed. " And the photograph ? " he said. " It would be a very simple matter to destroy it, and no one would be the wiser. Maretta might possibly be disappointed, but I could tell her it was a failure."

"Destroy it ? " cried Mrs. Seymour ; "and let the infernal villain escape after all ? Never! I wish one, at any rate, if only as a memento of the faithlessness of man."

Mrs. Nichols smiled a tired smile. " I shall expect you to send me the photograph as soon as possible, and to me only," she replied, with quiet dignity. " Come, Tom."

" Thank you very much," said Mr. Baker. " I am sure Maretta won't mind."

Two days later the photograph reached Mrs. Nichols at the breakfast-table, and on the following day Signor Spazzopalli left town. Society declared that he had been amusing himself with Miss Minerva Blair, and that he had gone away without offering himself to her. Society, feeling sure that this was so, gave a passing shrug of the shoulders, and forgot the affair before twenty-four hours had passed. Mrs. Duncan Seymour, however, was not so well off as society, in that she felt doubts on the subject but knew nothing. She compared notes with Mr. Irving K. Baker with unsatisfactory results. It appeared that Mrs. Nichols had not seen fit to inform either of them whether she had shown Minerva the photograph or not. Tom Nichols declared to his wife in the bosom of his family that this was fitting enough so far as Mrs. Seymour was concerned, but seemed rather severe on the author and originator of it all. But Elizabeth shook her head, and said:

"Irving K. Baker shall never know. You left it to me to decide whether to tell Minerva or not, and I mean to keep him wondering all the days of his life as to what really happened."